A Gilded Age Getaway

Blessings!

[signature]

A Gilded Age Getaway

The Back Inn Time Series

Book Five

Stephenia H. McGee

By The Vine Press

A Gilded Age Getaway
Copyright © 2023 by Stephenia H. McGee
Print Edition
www.StepheniaMcGee.com

Cover design: Roseanna White Designs
Model photography: Period Stock, LLC
Other images used under license from Shutterstock.com.

Library Cataloging Data
Names: McGee, Stephenia H. (Stephenia H. McGee) 1983 –
Title: A Gilded Age Getaway / Stephenia H. McGee
240p. 5 in. × 8 in.
Description: By The Vine Press digital eBook edition | By The Vine Press Trade paperback edition | Mississippi: By The Vine Press, 2023
Summary: Can one magical night of glamour in the past save their future?
Identifiers: ISBN-13: 978-1-63564-070-0 (trade) | 978-1-63564-067-0 (ebk.)
1. Christian Fiction 2. Time Travel Romance 3. Historical Romance 4. Clean and Wholesome Romance 5. Time Travel 6. Religious Fiction 7. Inspirational Romance

Dear reader,

As a historical fiction writer, I've always wondered what it would be like if I could travel back in time and get a firsthand glimpse of the eras I love to read about. Thus, the idea for this series was born. It's a fun way to imagine the impossible.

Please keep in mind, dear reader, that a *story* is all this is meant to be. It is not meant to spark a theological debate on whether God would allow the miracle of time travel. The Bible tells us "Man's days are determined; You [God] have decreed the number of his months and have set limits he cannot exceed" (Job 14:5) and "My times are in your hands" (Psalm 31:15).

Several of the things regarding the time travel in this story are not possible, but it allows us to suspend what we know to be true to simply enjoy the fictional freedom of the *what if...?* So, come with me, imaginative reader, and together let's go see what it might be like to "step back *inn* time and leave our troubles behind"!

Happy reading!
Stephenia

One

When had her life become so stale? And when—Fiona Robinson tugged at the skin next to her eye, leaning close to the bathroom mirror—had she started to get old? She groaned. Another wrinkle trying to set in. Yep. Old and boring.

The fiery woman with dreams of becoming an international food blogger no longer existed. Somewhere along the way she'd traded thoughts of jet-setting around the world for sixteen hundred square feet of suburban seclusion and a wardrobe containing more spit-up-stained shirts and worn jeans than skirts and high heels.

At least this morning she'd showered and put on a new outfit in honor of her mom's thoughtful gift of a weekend getaway for her and Tyler. But somehow, even this attempt at a romantic anniversary felt more like a chore than a present. She craved tingles of exhilaration. A burst of energy and excitement. Instead, she felt…tired.

When they'd wed, her husband had promised her that all Robinsons were adventurers. Swiss Family Robinson, Robinson Crusoe, even the space family—the one with the robot saying "danger, Will Robinson" were all destined for excitement. It was in the name, Tyler had said. A name she now shared with him. Tyler had promised an amazing adventure. She'd been caught up in the vision.

Yet ten years in and that sensation had grown cold.

These days her biggest adventures were trying to make it through the grocery store without someone having a tantrum. And ignoring the audacity of random strangers offering advice on how she could get her son to stop screaming if she bought him the candy bar he wanted. Most shot her a snarky side-eye like they could do better.

She swiped on mascara to bring life to her tired eyes and studied her reflection. Purplish rings on her pale skin evidenced all those busy hours spent with two rambunctious boys under five. One of whom seemed to think waking up at two o'clock this morning was a great game his mother and little brother needed to join in. Because Tyler had let the boys have a chocolaty dessert too late in the evening.

"Hey, love?" Tyler's voice drifted through the open double doors to their bedroom.

She still stood scowling at herself in the mirror. When had she changed from the fun-loving woman who jumped headfirst into marriage at twenty-three to the exhausted creature who could scarcely remember why she'd wanted this life in the first place?

"Where did you put my shoes?" Tyler's voice came closer. "You know, the brown ones?"

She leaned away from the mirror. "They are in the closet, right next to the—"

"Momma!" A little voice screeched from the kitchen, the wail carrying the distinct sound of sibling rivalry.

Fiona skirted past her husband and through the bedroom until her foot landed on something moist. Yuck! Who had left a half-eaten apple from breakfast on the carpet? She scooped up the fruit as her older son continued to howl. Then she stepped through the doorway and met a display that undid the hours of housework she'd accomplished last night after getting the boys tucked into bed.

Oh no.

With chocolate syrup smeared all over his face, Noah pointed at his little brother. "He did it!"

Why had she thought she could take a shower and get dressed while either of them were awake? Even with Tyler home. The man had a way of being here without, well, *being* here. A surge of frustration at her husband for not keeping an eye on them sent heat through her center. Pain throbbed at her temple. Why couldn't Tyler watch them for half an hour? She should have stayed up and taken a shower while they'd slept instead of trying to sneak in an hour of sleep. Then she could have been present to guard her clean house against toddler shenanigans.

Ethan sat on the tile floor, his two-year-old cherub face hosting wide eyes. Brown liquid smattered his pajamas and the entire space around him. He beamed. "Yummy!"

Despite the word, his face didn't bear evidence he'd partaken.

"Who got the syrup out of the pantry?" She frowned. "Wait. How did you even get to it?" She always kept risky items like sugar and syrups on the higher shelves, out of the reach of tiny hands.

Ethan used the chocolate as finger paint, creating a design across the tile floor. She hurried past the bar separating the living and dining space from the kitchen and snagged a roll of paper towels. Noah followed her, still whining that Ethan had somehow caused the trouble.

She wiped at the mess, which only gathered in the grout. She groaned. "Noah, how did you get the syrup?"

Big brown eyes stared at her. "I climbed."

"You what?" She whirled to look at the open pantry door, searching for how he'd managed the feat. And here she'd been lamenting about adventurers. "How?"

He puffed out his chest in his cowboy pajamas and tugged on her arm. A little brown handprint soiled her white blouse. "Here, Momma."

Grinning, he pointed at the industrial-sized box of cheese crackers she'd purchased when her mother-in-law had taken them to Sam's Club. How had the cardboard even held the boy up?

Noah scrambled onto the box, the feet on his one-piece pajamas marking a chocolate trail. "See?" He reached chest-level to one of the shelves. "I climbed, Momma. Got it here."

"I see." Except that was *not* the shelf for chocolate syrup. She cut an annoyed glance at the bedroom. Tyler must've put it there last night after he'd made the boys sundaes past bedtime.

She forced her lips into a semblance of serenity. "Noah, sweetie, we don't climb, okay? You can fall and get hurt."

His little chin trembled, brown eyes sorrowful. "I was gonna make you a treat."

"A treat?" She put her hands under his arms and scooped him from the box.

His nod flopped bangs she'd let grow to tame the cowlick that curled into his eyes. His lower lip poked out. "So you would want to stay here wif me."

Her heart wrenched. Maybe they shouldn't go. The boys were still so little. Noah tended to have separation anxiety, and Ethan...Uh-oh. Where was Ethan? He'd been quiet too long. Pulse ratcheting, she set Noah down and leaned over the bar to where she'd last seen the toddler in a pile of chocolate syrup and half-used paper towels.

Gone.

Tyler strolled out of the bedroom, phone to his head. He lifted his eyebrows at the mess, but never paused his conversation. He nodded toward the back door, telling her he would take the call outside. Where it was quieter.

It was their anniversary. He couldn't leave that phone for *one day*?

"Ethan?" With a growing sense of dread, she followed brown tracks from the dining space, through her bedroom doorway, and into her bathroom. Ethan sat on the floor, grinning as he painted a series of lines on the bathroom cabinets. Lovely artistic theme he had going. Mighty Chocolate versus Unsuspecting White Cabinets.

She'd warned Tyler that white trim was a bad idea. White *anything* was for people without kids. This was why she never wanted to have people over. She had one job caring for her home and boys. And she couldn't even do that well. How did those other moms look fit and styled all the time? Their homes probably looked like something out of a magazine. Even those career moms at church who always looked down on the stay-at-home types had to be doing a better job of wrangling their family's chaos.

Frustration mounting, she hefted her son from the bath mat, which earned an earsplitting howl and flailing arms. "No, Momma! Not done!"

And…so much for her white shirt. There should've been a soundtrack with a song about irony playing in the background. She settled the boy on her hip, headache blooming into a full-fledged pounding behind her right eye.

Then the doorbell rang. Ethan continued to cry while she bypassed the mound of chocolate-soaked paper towels and made her way to the front door.

Mom's eyes widened as Fiona flung back the stained oak. "Good morn—oh. Are you all right?"

Tears threatened, but Fiona pushed them back and forced an upturn to her lips. "Tyler left the chocolate syrup on a lower shelf. The boys thought it made good paint for my cabinets."

Little arms encircled her leg, and she looked down at Noah, who joined his voice with his brother's.

Mom's eyes glistened with sympathy. Dressed in practical jeans and a tee, she'd gathered her sunset-red curls into a cute updo somehow both fashionable and casual. How had she accomplished that when Fiona could barely keep her own red mane under control?

"Maybe this isn't a good idea." Fiona stepped aside, granting Mom a front-row view of this morning's disaster. "The boys are upset, and it will only get worse if I go. Besides, I have to clean all this up, and Tyler is…" She shook her head. "We should reschedule."

Mom gathered Ethan on her hip while she bent to free Noah's grip from Fiona's leg. The boy wouldn't budge. "Nonsense. This morning proves why I booked the room in the first place."

Right. Because Fiona was an utter failure at motherhood and her stagnant marriage had prompted her mother to make the four-hour trip to keep the boys and book a weekend retreat for Fiona and Tyler's tenth anniversary. Something neither of them would have done for themselves.

Tears burned again, and she swallowed them down. She *did* need a break. She glanced toward the glass patio door beyond the combined dining and living room space where she could see Tyler pacing in the backyard, hand moving around as he talked on the phone.

Mom followed her gaze but said nothing about her son-in-law. She focused on her grandchildren. "We are going to have so much fun! I brought crafts, and this afternoon, we are going to make our own snow cones!"

The last pronouncement caused Noah to let go of Fiona's leg. She shot Mom a grateful look. "Let me get this mess."

Fiona sponged up the chocolate syrup, then scrubbed the last of the stain from the grout. While she worked, Mom got both boys cleaned and dressed and began teaching them some type of game to get them to brush their teeth.

How did she do it? Fiona had to fight with Ethan to get the toothbrush in his mouth most days, and Noah barely tolerated the ritual, too concerned with returning to whatever he'd been playing with before she corralled him.

She dumped the last of the soiled paper towels into the garbage and headed back into her bathroom to remove Ethan's latest masterpiece. Finished, she washed her hands.

"There you are." Tyler shoved his phone into his back pocket as he rounded the corner. His smile slipped when he noticed her dishevelment. "What happened?"

She clamped her lips tight to keep from snapping that he had left the syrup within the boys' reach—*after* he had given them sugar right before bed. He, of course, had slept soundly while she'd tried to get two wired children to go back to sleep in the middle of the night.

"Were you going for the full ogre look?" he teased.

Heat erupted in her center and rocketed into her face. She was in no mood for the joke today. Her parents had decided that naming her after her fifth-something Irish great-grandmother was a beautifully unique idea. And maybe it would have been, if not for the fact that a movie came out when she was in middle school featuring a redheaded ogre princess named Fiona. A movie that became a franchise and left her with a joke that still hadn't gone away.

Tyler sobered and placed a hand on her shoulder. "What can I do to help?"

He meant it, and he was trying to be helpful. But stuffed-down resentment snarled feral fangs and wanted to bite. What could he do? He could have actually taken the day off. Like not answering the phone to deal with work calls kind of *day off.* Not just the kind where he basically worked from home. He could have been watching the boys. He could have cleaned up the mess, or—

"I got it." She stepped away from him before untamed thoughts became loose words. "Mom's here. But we need to tell her we can't go. You still have work calls, and the boys…"

"I had to take one call. But I'm finished." He flashed the grin that ten years ago had made her heart sputter. "Promise."

She wanted to believe him. Really she did. But experience had taught her that his company had no boundaries when it came to "work emergencies" on supposed vacation days. Tyler would answer if they called again, if only by sheer sense of duty. She understood—she did. His job provided for their family. But sometimes…sometimes, she wished she felt as important to him as that phone.

Laughter sounded from the kitchen, and she hung her head. Mom did such a great job with them.

Tyler's phone rang again. He gave her a pained look. "Won't take five minutes. I've got the boys while you change." He winked at her. "Then we'll hit the road."

He had the boys? Mom had the boys. He would be pacing around again outside. She gritted her teeth and turned toward the closet to find a clean outfit.

Anniversary trip, her foot. While Tyler worked—in all likelihood he'd packed his computer, too—she would bring a stack of books and find a place by herself on the beach. Just her, the waves, and the sand. Not bad, now that she thought of it.

Spending hours without anyone touching her, climbing on her, or demanding anything of her? Maybe this weekend was what she needed after all.

Two

Not again. Without being asked, Tyler's mother-in-law plucked Ethan from his arms with a rueful tip of her lips. Rebecca considered him a cad for taking calls on his anniversary. But she didn't understand what it meant to have the families of a hundred employees depending on him. He couldn't be completely unavailable. Not if he wanted to keep the company running and people employed. His father's retirement last year had left everything to him and his brother, John. The transition had been difficult, but he was getting a handle on things.

He put his wireless earbuds in and connected the call as he stepped through the front door to fetch Fiona's traveling pillow.

Rick didn't waste time on small talk. "Boss, I swear. He drove through the barrier. Not around it. *Through* it. Ain't our fault."

Tyler paused with his fingers on the minivan door handle. "What?"

"Then he smashed in his hood trying to drive onto bridge B. Fool didn't see the foot height difference in the concrete, I reckon. Now he's out here shouting at my guys about suing us."

Just what he needed. Some idiot totaling his car on the jobsite and trying to blame the company. "Has anyone called the police?"

"They should be coming."

Tyler wrenched open the minivan door and eyed the piles of toys, books, and... Was that a kitchen bowl? Good thing they were taking his truck and leaving Rebecca the van. "Make sure the officer sees where the guy ran past the road-closed barriers and puts that in the report."

"Not past them, Boss. *Through* them. He's gotta have scratches down both sides of that Mustang. Ain't no way he don't." Voices rose in the background, men shouting obscenities.

There. He plucked her pillow from the floorboard. "Get your crew away from him. Right now, all we have is an idiot who didn't obey construction signs and got himself into a mess. You let anyone on the crew flair his temper, and we'll—"

"Hey! Boss says get your—"

Tyler closed his eyes and shook his head. Rick's choice of words must have worked, however, because a second later he spoke back into the phone.

"Cop's here. I'll call you back when he's done."

"Make *sure* the report says the man drove through the barriers. Therefore, we aren't liable for any damage he sustained to his vehicle."

"You got it, Boss." The line went dead.

Fiona still hadn't come out. While he had a moment, Tyler stacked toys and books, then rolled out the shop vac. Cheerios, lost french fries, and who knew what else disappeared up the tube with a satisfying tumble. After he'd scrubbed every crumb from the carpet, he grabbed Fiona's back pillow and placed it in his pickup. He checked his watch. She should have had plenty of time to change by now. They needed to get on the road.

He opened the front door to his older son shouting. "No, Momma! Stay!"

In the kitchen, Noah clung to Fiona's legs. She looked up at the ceiling and drew a long breath. If he didn't swoop in to save the day, their chance at blissful days alone would go out the window.

He knelt and put a hand on the boy's small shoulder. "Hey, buddy. It's okay. Momma and I will only be gone for a bit. We will be home soon, and you'll have lots of fun with Nanna."

Tears rolled down the boy's round cheeks. "You go. Like always. Momma stay."

The words sliced through him. "That's because Daddy has to work. This time, he's taking Momma to do something fun. Don't you want Momma to have fun?"

Noah's eyes rounded, and he loosened his grasp. Tyler smiled at his progress. Before the sense of satisfaction could take hold, however, Noah flailed. "I wanna have fun too!"

Uh-oh. "You will. You'll be having fun with Nanna. Momma is going with me."

"No. I'm going with Momma too."

Tyler wasn't getting anywhere with this. He tugged Noah from Fiona's legs and lifted him. "Buddy. You're not going with us." His firm but gentle tone did nothing but make his son's lip poke out.

"Maybe we shouldn't go." Fiona frowned.

They needed this trip. The past year had been hard.

"Noah's my big boy." Time for a different tactic. "He's going to take good care of Nanna while we're gone." He spoke to Fiona. "You don't have to worry about leaving Nanna. We can trust Noah to take good care of her."

Noah looked at his grandmother in the kitchen, Ethan propped on her hip with his pudgy hands tangled in her hair.

"You'll take good care of Nanna for us, won't you?"

His gaze darted between his mother and grandmother. His chin dipped in a reluctant nod.

Crisis averted. "That's my boy. I knew I could count on you." Tyler swung Noah into the air and elicited a giggle before placing him on the floor.

Determined feet padded across the tile as he rounded the barstools. "Nanna, my daddy says I have to take care of you."

Tyler winked at Fiona and gestured toward the door. When she hesitated, a line forming between her brows, he leaned close. "Let's go while they're distracted."

"Without telling them goodbye?"

Her sharp whisper drew Rebecca's notice. His mother-in-law gave them a nod toward the door. She continued to hold Noah's attention with talk about snow cones and crafts while swaying Ethan on her hip.

Tyler took his wife's hand and urged her to uproot from the tile. After a few heartbeats and a look of guilt toward Rebecca, she followed him outside.

As soon as he shut the door, she stopped to stare at it. "Are you sure about this? Won't they be even more upset when they realize we snuck out?"

Rebecca could handle it. "They'll be fine."

Her lips scrunched, and her features clouded. If she went back now, they might as well cancel. He waited. Then she sucked in a breath and marched to the minivan.

"I already got your pillow."

"Oh. Thanks." She slid open the van door and stopped. "But I'm looking for Ethan's... Did you vacuum?"

At least he could do something right. "Sure did."

Her brows pinched together. "I haven't had time. I spent most of the night trying to clean the house."

She'd been up cleaning the house? Why in the…? Never mind. He'd leave that one alone. He knew she hadn't had time to clean the van. That's why he'd done the job for her. "I did it while I was waiting on you to change. Didn't take long."

Her body stiffened. "I'm sure. Especially when someone else has the children."

What did she mean by that? He held his tongue, not wanting to get into an argument about vacuuming the van. Not like that time he'd made the mistake of starting a load of his laundry when he'd run out of boxers. Somehow, doing so had meant he thought his wife was a failure. He still hadn't quite figured that out.

"I need to give Mom Ethan's blankie. He won't nap without it."

Hadn't the boy slept all night just fine with the blanket still in the van? "Then leave it hanging on the doorknob and text her where it is."

She headed toward the front door. "And I forgot my books."

"Why do you need books?"

A glint flickered in her eyes before it faded. "So I'll have something to do."

He shrugged off the barb. "We'll have plenty to do. If you go back in, you might not get back out."

After what had to be a full minute, she hung the

blanket on the doorknob and then opened the passenger door without a word. Tyler hopped in, cranked the engine, and backed out of the driveway before she could change her mind. His phone rang before they made it out of the neighborhood.

Anger radiated off his wife in acidic waves. The muscle in his jaw twitched. He should let it go to voicemail. Someone else could handle whatever crisis came next.

"Just take it." Her resigned words landed like an uppercut.

The screen on the dash showed Rick's contact again. Probably telling him about the police report. But he might need to make sure Rick didn't let Mustang Guy do anything else stupid. "Some of the field guys don't know I'm out today. They call straight to me instead of into the office."

She faced the window and mumbled something about how she should have gone back for the books. His phone continued to play the factory-set tune he'd never bothered changing. She'd be mad at him either way. He needed to make sure he put this situation to bed so he wouldn't be worrying about it the rest of the day. He'd make it up to her.

With a huff, he connected the call. "This is Tyler."

"What do you want me to do with this report?" Rick shouted something at one of the crew about unloading a pipe in the wrong place. Good thing he still had one of his earbuds in.

"Take it to Kelly. That way we'll have a copy on file at the office if he tries to make any claims on us."

Fiona had picked up her phone, ignoring him. So, for the next twenty minutes, Tyler went over the delayed rebar shipment and the grades for the bridge end abutments and promised to get in touch with the concrete supplier on Monday to schedule a pour for next week. "If you need anything else today, call John. I'm out of the office."

"Sure thing, Boss."

They ended the call, and Tyler slid the button to vibrate. "Sorry about that. We had a guy drive his car through the road-closure signs. Then he hit the end of the bridge and wants to blame us for it."

She looked up from scrolling Pinterest. "He hit the end of the bridge?"

"Drove right into a one-foot lift. After he had to pass the roller and a dozer to do it."

She shook her head. "People are crazy."

"Especially since he's threatening to sue us for damages to his car."

"Wow. You can't make this stuff up." She chuckled and dropped her phone in the cup holder. Then she rubbed at her temples. "Do you think the boys will be okay?"

"They'll be fine. Your mom is great with them."

"Yeah." She slathered the word with dejection.

Better steer this conversation away from her worrying about the boys. "It was really nice of her to give us this trip. I'm looking forward to spending some quality time with you."

She shifted her body back toward him. "Really?"

Why did she sound so surprised? "Things have been hectic lately. It'll be nice to get back to us for a while." He attempted a sultry look. "Kindle the romance."

Her face softened, and she turned those gorgeous eyes on him, her flirtatious gaze sparking a fire in his gut. "It would."

He reached across the console to take her hand. She offered him a gentle squeeze. He was thinking of a quip to remind her of the "us time" they'd had on their honeymoon and how they could try for the ten-year encore performance when his phone rang again. His brother's contact number lit up the screen on his truck's dash. John knew Tyler had today off, so if he was calling, it had to be important.

Fiona freed her hand from his, all hints of playfulness gone. She plucked her phone from the cup holder and shifted her shoulders toward the window.

Guilt pulled at him as he reached for the console screen and connected the call.

When he got back from the coast, he'd throttle his brother.

Three

$\mathcal{A}$t least the house was pretty. The Victorian mansion nestled in the embrace of ancient oaks. Hanging moss swayed from the branches. A spring breeze brought the briny scent of the nearby ocean, but Fiona couldn't see any water from here. She would have preferred a beach view, but of course, she'd never tell Mom.

The front door popped open as Tyler dropped their suitcases in the driveway. A woman bustled out, halting Fiona's contemplation about which swing on the wraparound front porch would be best for lounging.

"Uh, wow." Tyler paused with one suitcase handle half-extended. "Wonder where she's going."

The woman wore an elaborate gown of cascading silk, hues of blue and green overlapping one another in at least a dozen places. Her gray curls piled onto her head, and an intricate mask of swirling peacock feathers and fabric covered the top part of her face.

"Must be some kind of costume party."

"In March?" Tyler shook his head and righted the suitcases, pulling one in each hand. "Is she doing a Mardi Gras thing?"

Wherever the woman was headed, she'd be having a lot of fun dressed like that. Fiona ignored the longing nipping her heart. They passed a sign for the house that said something about stepping back "inn" time—how clever—and took the short walk to the porch steps. The oddly dressed woman still hadn't moved from where she stood like a queen presiding over her court.

"Mr. and Mrs. Robinson! Welcome, welcome." The woman swept her hand out, showing off elbow-length white gloves.

Tyler and Fiona exchanged a glance. This wasn't part of the weekend package, was it? Excitement tingled through her. Had Mom found some kind of themed resort? Now *that* would be interesting. And totally worth skipping a beach view.

"Uh, we're supposed to be checking into The Depot. Is this the right place?" His doubtful gaze swept over the woman blocking the door, to the sign behind him, and back to the peacock lady again.

Amusement tugged at her lips. "This is precisely where you are supposed to be, Mr. Robinson." She lifted her eyebrows at Fiona as though sharing some kind of secret. "Come in. I have your room ready."

Politeness dictated she shouldn't ask why the woman wore such an outfit, but... "Is there a costume party happening this weekend, or do you dress this way for tours?" Weren't there houses in Natchez where the hostesses wore period costumes to give tours to their guests?

"This is for the ball, of course."

Ball? "There's a party?"

The woman sashayed inside, her heels clicking over a polished hardwood floor. "The grandest ball ever seen, some say."

An exaggeration for an uneventful seaside town in Mississippi, but the woman's enthusiasm sparked Fiona's curiosity. "Oh, what fun. Is the party just for guests?"

Her bright-red lips curved beneath the extravagant mask. "Both, you might say."

Fiona cut a look at Tyler, but he didn't notice. Too busy frowning at something on his phone. "I wish I'd known to bring a costume."

They followed the woman down a hallway and into a well-appointed library. She motioned them inside. "Not to worry, dear. Everything you need has already been provided."

Wow. Maybe Mom had found a themed weekend. And she'd had enough foresight to have costumes made for them? What a cool surprise.

Inside the library, floor-to-ceiling shelves supported leather-bound books. So she didn't have to worry about leaving hers at home after all.

The mysterious woman opened a tome on the mahogany desk. Her eyes sparkled. "Oh my. This is special indeed."

"What is?"

Tyler now held his phone toward the ceiling. He lowered it when he caught her look. "No service."

She forced herself not to roll her eyes and maintained a pleasant expression for their hostess.

"Oh, just something I haven't gotten to do in a long time." The lady moved on without further explanation. "Now that you're all checked in, let's get you up to your room. You'll need time to get ready for the ball. It's not to be missed."

"Ball?" Tyler lowered his phone. "What are you talking about?"

Fiona unclenched her jaw, but her words still snapped more than she intended. "If you'd been paying attention, you would know."

He stashed the phone, his shoulders inching up.

They would never enjoy the party if they started fighting, so she smothered her irritation. "There's a costume party here tonight. Part of the package Mom got us."

A line formed between his dark brows. "We didn't bring any costumes."

"This lady…" She nodded to the woman waiting at the door for them. "Um, I'm sorry. What was your name again?"

"Mrs. Easley."

"Mrs. Easley said everything we need is already here." She grinned, despite her annoyance at her husband's dubious look. "Won't that be so much fun?"

Her excitement must have rubbed off on him because the frown eased. "Whatever makes you happy, love."

Bless him. He could still be sweet when he wanted. If only he weren't so distracted all the time.

"Perfect." Mrs. Easley made another grand gesture toward the hall. "Let's get going, then. Shall we?"

They followed her up a curving staircase to the second floor. Paintings of different time periods hung over the carpeted hall—a wagon train, the Boston Tea Party, some kind of princess with a castle, a girl in a chef hat and apron outside a mansion, and even a fifties-era photograph of an Air Force base. Talk about eclectic.

They stopped at the last room in the hall. Hopefully, all the rest of these rooms were filled as well, or it might be a dull party.

"Here we are. Number fifteen." Mrs. Easley thrust a black metal key into the antique keyhole and twisted it. As the door swung open on silent hinges, she held the key out to Tyler.

Fiona stepped inside. A four-poster bed supporting a canopy with sweeping curtains like a grown-up version of a blanket fort claimed center court. Beyond it, a beast of a wardrobe dominated the left wall, and windows to the right overlooked a backyard offering a quaint fountain, cozy sitting areas, and abundant plants.

"You'll find your attire in the wardrobe." Mrs. Easley pointed at the carved piece of furniture fit for that castle painting. "I highly suggest donning your outfits prior to retrieving your invitation. Otherwise, things could get a bit awkward."

Without explaining herself, Mrs. Easley closed the door and left them.

"That was weird." Tyler wheeled their suitcases to the end of the bed and surveyed the king-sized mattress. He wiggled his brows. "How about we stay in instead?"

And miss the first real date they'd had in the past year? Not a chance. "Mom paid for all of this. I want to experience what she has planned."

"You're right." He turned to the wardrobe. "So let's see what kind of funky getup your mom has for us." He opened the wardrobe and pulled out a knee-length deep-blue jacket. "Hmm. Looks like I'm going to be a…pirate?"

Fiona almost rolled her eyes thinking he was mistaking a historical evening suit for a pirate costume until he showed her the ruffled white shirt, tight pants, knee-high boots, and sword. Maybe it was a costume ball.

He replaced the jacket and grabbed a feminine coppery fabric. "And you're a…huh. I don't know. What's this supposed to be?"

She took a floor-length, high-waisted dress with

puffed sleeves and examined the shimmering material. "Regency-era gown, if I had to guess. See how it opens down the front? There should be another piece to it that this goes over. Should look like a fancy petticoat." At his raised eyebrows, she added, "A nightgown-looking thing."

"Yeah. Here." He handed her a white gown with delicate embroidery.

She ran her fingers over the textures. "So pretty."

"That color will look good on you." He nodded to the copper-and-brown piece with the same floor-length hemline and embroidery as the petticoat. "Why don't you try it on?"

Maybe she'd be getting an adventure after all. Taking the pieces, she hurried to the bathroom to change. White tile lined the space, and she'd love a leisurely soak in that claw-foot tub.

The creamy white dress fit perfectly. The outer gown slid on like a jacket and buttoned with a neat enclosure just under her breasts. Regency, for sure. Made sense. This place was all about stepping back "inn" time, and with those paintings from different eras lining the halls, all the guests for this party likely wore costumes from history. But this gown sure wasn't some cheap Halloween-store knockoff. How much had Mom spent on this thing?

She stepped out of the bathroom with a swish of shimmering fabric. "Well, what do you think?"

A billowy white shirt hung open at his throat. Tyler's sword clattered as he fastened a wide belt around his hips. Then his fingers stilled, and he let out a low whistle. "Whoa. Cool. You look great, love."

He sure was handsome in that pair of tight pants and open-neck shirt. Warmth tingled through her as he watched her snag bobby pins from her suitcase and wander over to the desk nestled between the windows. She lifted a white mask decorated with golden sparkles and gold and brown feathers. "Hmm, apparently, we are supposed to wear masks. Wow. This looks like something from Carnival of Venice." She ran a finger over a black leather mask like Zorro's. "Yours is a bit more…rugged."

Behind her, he laughed. "I'll take that over sparkly, thanks."

She returned to the bathroom and swept her red curls to one side of her neck, securing the look with pins. Then she placed the mask on her face—another impeccable fit—and tucked the strings inside her hair. There. Perfect.

"Wow." He paused in pulling on a pair of knee-high black boots as she stepped back into the room.

Her stomach fluttered in a way it hadn't in a while. She ducked her head and smoothed a hand over the shimmery fabric. "Thanks."

They were totally going to have to send Mom pictures. She found a pair of comfortable brown flats in the bottom of the wardrobe. *Thanks, Mom, for not giving me a pair of heels!* Aching feet would ruin the evening.

At scraping metal, she spun back to her husband. He slid the curved sword out of its scabbard and examined the blade. "Where'd she get all this stuff?"

"Who cares where she got it? But you can bet she will be getting a *huge* thank you." As soon as they finished dressing, she'd get Mrs. Easley to take a picture on her phone. "She must have been planning this awhile."

He clattered the sword back into the scabbard, then scooped up his Zorro mask.

What time did everything start? They should have thought about supper before getting dressed. She returned to the writing desk and picked up the invitation. "Wow, the theme is the New York Vanderbilt Ball of 1883."

"Vanderbilt? Like the superrich, founded-the-college-in-Nashville Vanderbilt?" Tyler lifted his arms. "Then why am I dressed like a pirate?"

Fiona shrugged. "Probably just a gimmick. As long as you are dressed from some point in history, it counts."

A headache started behind her temple so suddenly that she swayed. Whoa. What was happening? Her vision blurred, and the room spun.

Tyler rushed to her side and slipped an arm around her waist. "Fiona?" His voice, pitched up a notch, echoed in her thudding head. "Are you all right?"

Not really. She'd nearly fainted. She blinked, trying to clear her vision. "Yeah. My head…" She swallowed.

"You better lie down."

She didn't want to miss the party.

The room started to swim, the pain behind her eyes intensifying. She opened her mouth to concede, but her lips fumbled over the words.

Tyler shifted next to her and let out a groan. Somewhere in the back of her mind, an alarm sounded.

She stumbled, and the two of them landed in a heap on the ground. Then everything went black.

Four

Fiona groaned as Tyler pulled her to standing. Her legs tangled in the long dress, and she wobbled before steadying herself. She blinked hard, and the headache receded as quickly as it had started, leaving her mind clear. Totally weird.

"Are you all right?" He frowned, his brown eyes intense as they searched hers for answers.

"Yeah. You?" She returned his scrutiny. She could have sworn he'd gotten woozy too.

He shook his head, running his hands down the white pirate shirt. "I guess. That was weird. I got dizzy and then…"

"Did we both black out?" Her stomach curdled as she followed her husband's gaze. Her pulse skittered. "Uh, where are we?"

This *wasn't* the hotel room they'd checked into. Similar, with antique furniture in dark hues and a wardrobe for hanging clothes, but this one dwarfed the other. Rich, wine-colored curtains flanked a picture window, and a thick carpet cushioned her feet.

"Did we wander over to another room? I don't remember doing that. Do you?" Her heart rate accelerating, she scurried to the window.

What she saw below choked off her breath. "Um…Tyler?"

He darted to her side, his face hovering over her shoulder. "What in the world?"

She could only gape. At least four stories below, wide brick streets teemed with horse-drawn carts, men in suits, and women dressed in tailored historical gowns. She pressed her face against the glass, the absurdity disappearing behind the fog she created on the pane.

"I don't remember those buildings. Do you remember those buildings?" Tyler jabbed a finger at the window, an alarmed undercurrent rushing beneath his punctuated words.

They were no longer on the quiet street lined with oaks dripping with airy moss. Instead, massive buildings from an era when architecture had class stood like regal giants overlooking the well-dressed people.

She gripped Tyler's arm. "Are you seeing this?"

He gawked. "We need to call your mom."

Mom? Why would they call…? Fiona shook the cobwebs forming in her brain. "Right. She set this up." She scanned the room for their suitcases. "Where's your phone?" He never went anywhere without it.

He patted his hips and back pocket. "I must have

left it in the other room."

"I don't see my purse or our suitcases, either." Fighting down her anxiety, she wrenched open the door and dashed out. Rooms lined both sides of another long hall, though the ornately carved molding and polished floors were not that of the inn they'd checked into.

A teen wearing a dark-blue cotton dress and a crisp white apron stepped out from one room and closed the door behind her. She might work here, especially given the historical look of what appeared to be a maid's uniform.

Fiona raised her hand. "Excuse me!"

The girl bustled her way. "Yes, miss?"

"Where is Mrs. Easley?"

Long lashes blinked over blue eyes. "I'm sorry, miss. I don't know of a guest by that name. Perhaps you should inquire in the lobby?"

"No, she owns the hotel. The Depot."

The girl pursed her lips. "You are in the Fifth Avenue Hotel."

"Fifth...like *New York*?" Fiona put a hand to her face, just now noticing she no longer wore the costume mask.

The girl's eyebrows rose before she lowered them in suspicion. "Of course." She then took a hesitant step closer. "Are you in need of help?"

This couldn't be happening. New York? The scene outside the window. All of it sent Fiona's stomach twisting like a tornado. There had to be an explanation. This couldn't all be an elaborate charade for the Vanderbilt-themed party could—?

"Are you here for the event?" The girl motioned at Fiona's dress. "'Tis a right fine costume. I've heard the ladies will be wearing all manner of ensembles tonight. Some from exotic places or bygone eras. Others"—she leaned closer, gushing out excitement—"are rumored to be coming as types of animals. Can you imagine?"

Fiona's mind whirled. The costumes. The ball. New York. If she remembered correctly, the Vanderbilt mansion on Fifth Avenue would host an expensive ball to impress the New York society's "old money" and launch the wealthy family into the famous 400.

And Dad said she wouldn't learn anything from reading those historical romance books.

"Um…" She twisted her fingers in her dress, about to sound like an idiot. "You wouldn't happen to be talking about the Vanderbilt ball…" She cringed. "Of, uh, 1883…would you?"

The girl's eyes lit, sending dread into Fiona's stomach. "The city can talk of nothing else." She stepped closer. "I'm hoping to leave early enough to catch a glimpse of the 400 in some of their costumes." Her eyebrows dipped even further in thought. "You aren't one of that set, though…are you? Not to offend. It's only that…"

The girl's words faded to mumbles. Mouth arid,

Fiona could only nod as the girl twittered on, the words scarcely audible over the pounding in her ears. Were they—no. They couldn't be.

Could they? The streets outside the window, this hall…all so different. She raised her hand, stalling the maid's gushing about dresses and fashionable gentlemen. "It's 1883."

The girl giggled at the absurd statement without the first hint of ridicule. "Yes, miss. The Vanderbilt's party is the event of the year for certain."

Tyler appeared at her side and gripped her elbow. The girl bobbed a curtsy and said something about getting back to work before scurrying down the hallway. They stood there in stunned silence until Tyler held something out to her.

"I found this. Read it."

She took the folded paper and opened the single sheet.

Dear Mr. and Mrs. Robinson,

What a delightful experience you have in store for you this evening. Some say the Vanderbilt ball of 1883 was the event of the century. It was known to spark the imagination and send its attendees into a magical night of romance. Something, I suspect, is exactly what you two need. Do not fear. You will not be gone any longer than you planned. No need to worry over the little ones. Like Cinderella, you will get to enjoy the ball and find your romance, but you will soon return.

Come and find me at the mansion. It is not often I get to participate in my guests' adventures, and I have more to share.

Your friend,
Mrs. Easley

Fiona read the letter two more times before meeting her husband's stare. "This has to be some kind of elaborate show for the theme of her party."

He nodded, though doubt glimmered in his gaze. "Yeah." He scratched the back of his neck. "Except, well, then how do you explain what we saw outside?"

Or what the girl had said about them being in 1883. The only explanation Fiona could fathom was simply impossible. So impossible she couldn't give the absurd idea credence by voicing it.

"She said she's going to be at the party." The muscle in the side of Tyler's jaw ticked the way it did whenever he struggled to hold back emotions behind a calm façade. "I'm guessing that's where we're going to find answers."

Fiona folded the letter. "Why does she mention the boys? Do you think they're okay?" An urge to call her mother had her palms sweating. "We need to find a phone and check on them."

Tyler jerked his head in agreement. "There should be one downstairs."

After searching and detouring down various hallways—where they encountered more people garbed in historical outfits who gave them strange looks—they located a stairway. Ahead of them, an older couple walked with the unhurried gait of those not in crisis.

"I don't see why we couldn't have tried the vertical railway, Harold." A woman in a floor-length gown and a gaudy hat the size of a serving platter spoke with a bored tone as she looped her hand over the older gentleman's outstretched arm.

Fiona eyed the couple taking the stairway ahead of them. What in the world was a vertical railway? She and Tyler neared, forced to slow their pace.

"I do not trust that contraption, my dear. What need have we of a conveyance to see us down to the ground floor? It's hardly a tax on the body."

Tyler leaned close as they tried to keep a respectable distance behind the other couple. "Are they talking about an elevator?"

The words in the letter niggled in her mind, but she shrugged. They continued down the stairway, passing under fancy crystal lights flickering with gas flames. The sensation that they were no longer in the present pressed down on her with every step toward the ground floor. Even hotels wanting to show off a historical flair wouldn't go without modern lights.

And she hadn't seen a single power outlet. Not to mention the way every single person dressed. Or the way they talked. Unless she and Tyler had stumbled upon the world's most elaborate production, they appeared to have been transported to the past. But how? This couldn't be happening.

Her suspicions only gained steam when they descended into a wide room with soaring ceilings where the people all wore formal-looking attire.

God. This is crazy. Like, really, really crazy. Are you seeing this? Right. You're everywhere. Even in 1883. In New York City. Where you, of course, can be but I shouldn't be. And what about the boys? Going to the coast was one thing. New York is totally different.

The faster the frenzied prayer swirled through her mind the more her pulse skyrocketed. Tyler pulled her along to a counter where he argued with a man about finding a pay phone. The flustered man in glasses said something about Tyler going to a telegraph center.

We need to go home, God. I'm not Cinderella. I know I said I wanted an adventure, but...

Peace enveloped her. The boys were safe at home with her mother. She'd wanted an adventure. Something amazing. A night of romance and excitement. And just like the words of Ephesians 3:20, God had proven that he would do more than she could ever ask or think.

When Tyler grumbled something and turned to leave, she tugged his hand before he'd made it more than a dozen steps, drawing him to an abrupt halt. "Tyler. Wait."

Above them, the towering ceiling rose two stories over their heads, elaborate in detail. What a wonder they had stumbled into. "I think…" She fit her hands to her hips, crinkling silk and willing herself to appear confident. "I think God granted us a miracle. I prayed for an adventure." She lifted her chin. "And, well, this is it."

Tyler waved a hand. "*What* is it?"

His cautionary voice pricked her assurance, but she squared her shoulders. "We've grown stale. Our marriage feels more like being roommates than spouses. I'm tired and worn out. So are you. We have nothing left to give one another at the end of the day."

The corners of his eyes tightened, and he opened his mouth. But she laid her hands on his chest, stepping closer to capture his full attention.

"I prayed for a miracle. A grand romantic adventure. That is what we got. I get to be Cinderella. You are my handsome prince. And for one night, we get to experience the extraordinary."

Tyler stiffened. His jaw twitched, and conflict warred behind his eyes. He opened his mouth. Closed it. Opened it again. "I love your passion and imagination."

Sensing a "but" coming, she braced herself.

"But we need to find a phone and call your mom. Check on the boys. Then we need to find that weird lady and figure out what is going on."

He was right. She was a terrible mother. She should be panicking. Worried about her children. Making sure they got home to their babies. She shouldn't be fantasizing about accepting a miracle and enjoying a night of romance when —

"I don't have time for this right now."

Wait. What? An internal heat charred the agreement she'd been about to voice. The peace she'd found earlier sizzled away.

"You don't have *time*?" The word came out as nearly a screech. People eyed them, and her face heated. She lowered her voice. "Of course, you don't. You never have time for us."

That wasn't true. Not really. Tyler loved her and the boys. But after months of holding in her frustration and her ridiculous jealousy of the attention he showed his job, the words exploded like shrapnel, injuring her target with every cutting accusation.

A part of her screamed out a warning, but her mouth kept going. "You care more about that job than you do your family."

The pain she expected erupted in his eyes, and she stepped back from him, unshed tears burning. She'd wanted to say those things to him. To break through the wall so he could finally *see*. But now that she had, she wished she could call them back.

Five

No one knew better how to wound him than his beautiful bride. Tyler stood in the middle of a fancy hotel, surrounded by onlookers while dressed like a pirate. Yet none of that mattered as he faced the woman to whom he'd pledged his heart and his life.

Did she doubt his love for her? Had he let himself become so concerned with everything he needed to accomplish that he'd leaned too heavily on the foundation he'd thought they had—and let that weight cause their marriage to crumble? He knew she'd been tired lately. Had sensed her pulling away.

"Fiona, I…" The words deteriorated before they formed. What could he say?

She brushed tears from her eyes. "I shouldn't have said that. I didn't mean—"

"Yeah, you did." After a decade of marriage, he knew his wife. She hadn't wanted to say the words. Regretted letting them fly free. But she'd meant them.

He had failed her. But the middle of a crisis wasn't

the time to deal with their emotional issues. "I know you've been unhappy with me, but right now, we need to find a way out of here."

Her vulnerable expression shuttered behind a mask of cold indifference, and another jab landed in his gut.

"Of course. We need to find Mrs. Easley if we are going to learn anything. I have a feeling phones here aren't going to be able to let us call home." She turned up her nose. "Or your office."

He clamped his teeth against a retort. "We need to look at this logically."

"I am." She crossed her arms. "Logically, we are in a different hotel. Logically, there are people everywhere dressed from a different time. *Logically*, the city outside of those doors isn't the quiet Mississippi town we are supposed to be in."

Annoyance flared at her sarcastic tone. "What are you saying, then? That we've traveled back in time? To *New York*? That's ridiculous."

She huffed. "You have a better explanation?"

He didn't, and that had him anxious. He let out a slow breath through his nose. "We need to think this through."

"As impossible as it seems," she whispered, "we were given the gift of one extraordinary night. A chance to save *us*."

They needed saving? The words hit him like a pallet of bricks. Consumed with the everyday disasters, had he failed to notice how bad things were at home? Ice settled in his stomach.

I could use some wisdom here, Lord.

Husbands, love your wives. Giving yourself up for her.

He shivered at the parts of Ephesians 5:25 they'd studied years ago in a couples' Sunday school class.

Grinding his teeth, he relaxed his clenched fingers. He did love her. Why did she think he stressed over keeping the company afloat? He'd promised to provide for her if she ever decided to stay home with their children, and he would sacrifice every ounce of his stamina to do so.

He couldn't take one more ounce of pressure. He needed God to give him encouragement, not condemnation.

A man shall leave his father and his mother and hold fast to his wife. Tyler rubbed his temples, thoughts churning. Surely God didn't want him to leave his family's business. He hadn't felt led to quit his job. But maybe God was saying he had been holding too fast to his work and, in so doing, had been letting his wife slip through his fingers.

Had God worked some kind of extraordinary miracle? Maybe he was in a coma and none of this was real. Maybe God was giving him a type of dream/vision thing to show him what he needed to do in real life.

Every sound, smell, and assault on his senses screamed that he stood in a real place. Either way, maybe it didn't matter. Maybe he needed to set aside the current crisis and focus on Fiona.

Are you saying I should accept this craziness, God?

This is the day the Lord has made, and I shall rejoice and be glad in it.

Seemed his mind had a Bible verse for every question. At least he was getting answers. God certainly had a sense of humor.

He pulled Fiona to him. She stiffened, then melted into his chest as though she'd been longing to do so. As she held fast to him, he stroked her fiery hair, reminded of the way he'd always loved her passion. Fiona never did anything in halves. The thought of her impassioned heart turning cold toward him filled him with dread.

They stood there as passersby gave them scandalized looks. He didn't care. How long had it been since he'd stood still and held his wife? She was right. They needed time together. Time to reconnect.

That's what had made him so grateful for his mother-in-law's anniversary gift. He still needed answers and intended to locate the enigmatic Mrs. Easley to get them, but he'd take the odd circumstances and use them to win his wife.

"I'm sorry, love." He whispered against her temple. "You always come first. Even if I have failed at showing you that."

She leaned away from him, her luminous eyes searching his. "I know you love us. And I love you. But lately, I've felt so…alone."

He closed his eyes against the hurt and nodded. "I'll do better." How he'd accomplish that, when so many things demanded his time, he had no idea.

No one is demanding your time right now.

The thought slammed into him. Hadn't he wished for time off where no one called him? When no issues erupted that his brother couldn't handle? And here God had granted that. His phone wouldn't work. No internet to log on to. No email, no texts.

For one strangely beautiful day, all the distractions, obligations, and responsibilities were gone. As long as they could get back home to the boys on Sunday, then he had no reason not to accept the miracle. Even if doing so went against his analytical nature.

He took her hand and looped it over his arm. "Looks like we have an adventure on our hands. Care to join me in exploring New York?" The words felt silly, but the reward of the sparkle returning to her eyes made up for it.

Then the joyous spark dimmed. "Do you think the boys are okay?"

"They're with your mom. Regardless of where—or *when*—we are, we know that for sure. So as long as we go home as scheduled, everything should be fine."

He hoped.

Everything would be fine. Fiona prayed those words would prove true as they stepped from the hotel and onto a busy and rather smelly street. The piles of manure on the road clashed with the formal dress of those they passed. People eyed them.

No wonder. Fiona wore a gown from the wrong era, and her husband looked like a pirate. She couldn't look more out of place among feathered hats and bustled gowns than if she'd shown up here in her jeans and blouse.

Well, okay. That might not be true. Still. "Where do you think the party is?"

Tyler tugged his gaze away from the bustling street. "Vanderbilt mansion. Shouldn't be too hard to find."

Sure enough, after flagging down a gentleman in a well-made suit and asking where to find the Vanderbilt home for tonight's party, they had straightforward directions. Keep walking up Fifth Avenue until they hit Fifty-Second Street.

Tyler's steps slowed. "That's going to be a long walk. What time does the ball start?"

"I have no idea. It didn't say." She shrugged, then tapped a finger on her lips. "I read a book once where the characters went to this ball. I'm pretty sure it's late at night."

Her husband nodded. He wouldn't have anything better to go on. She gestured back toward the hotel. "We should get that invitation and our masks. We might need them. Then let's find Mrs. Easley."

By the time they made their way through the lobby, back up the stairs, and to the room where they'd left the door standing open, Fiona had begun to accept the circumstances and foster excitement.

"Isn't this cool? I mean, yeah, it's weird and all. But it's cool, right?"

Tyler grunted. Then, as though thinking better of it, he plastered on a smile. "It's interesting, that's for sure."

He still looked worried. Who could blame him?

They snagged their masks from the desk, and he tucked both inside the inner pocket of his jacket. The long tails flapped behind him, and the way his pants tucked into knee-high boots was cute.

"Anything else we should take?" He patted the sword at his side like he thought he might need to use the thing.

She had no idea. Just to be sure, she checked the wardrobe and around the room but found nothing. After he pocketed the invitation along with the masks, they returned to the lobby.

Outside, the day's shadows lengthened into late afternoon, and she shivered. Despite the full sunshine, the temperature dipped below her comfort range. Too bad she didn't have a coat. Or the long sleeves of every other woman they passed along the sidewalks. She shivered anew, her open collarbone and exposed arms making her feel scandalous.

Though most of the feeling stemmed from the looks people kept giving them.

"How far did you say we had to walk?"

"We are on Thirty-First Street. The Vanderbilt house is on Fifty-Second."

The road didn't resemble anything like the famed Fifth Avenue shopping district. There were big buildings, yes. And plenty had to be stores. But without all the gaudy signs and neon lights, who could tell?

"That makes about twenty blocks." Good thing she had flats instead of heels. "Maybe we can hire a taxi carriage."

Tyler looked out over the mess of vehicles traveling the road with men on horseback darting in between wagons parked with no sense of order. "Which ones are those?"

"They're called hansom cabs." Score another point for romance novels.

"Okay, great. Which ones are those?"

She had no idea.

She must've looked confused because he shrugged. "Let's walk. If it doesn't start until night, we have plenty of time and lots to see."

A sense of adventure welling once more, she clasped his hand, and they headed down the street. They walked in silence, falling in among the throngs clogging the sidewalks. Ornate buildings, some marked as businesses while others had the distinct look of homes, towered over both sides of the road. She'd read about the Gilded Age, but nothing prepared her for this. Opulence erupted from every gold-trimmed carriage to pressed suit to marble façade.

She sucked in a deep breath.

Then nearly choked on the manure odor.

How could this place be both so beautiful and stinky? At least they had sidewalks so she could avoid the gunk. How much longer until cars hit the road?

"No honking horns like in the movies," she quipped.

Tyler chuckled. "No yellow taxis, no horns, no drivers shouting obscenities. It is weirdly quiet."

"A lot more peaceful than modern times. And no neon lights and flashing ads."

"Right. Just horse turds and clopping hooves."

"Stop there, sir." A man stepped into their path and held up a gloved hand. His blue coat with a row of brass buttons and flat-topped hat marked him as a police officer. He laid his other hand on the club at his side. "Planning on causing trouble in this district?"

"What?" Tyler shook his head.

She leaned closer. "It's the sword."

Tyler gripped the hilt of the costume weapon, and the police officer shifted into a fighting stance before

Tyler threw up his hands. "Sorry! No. I'm a pirate."

The officer pulled the club from his belt.

Fiona touched Tyler's arm. "It's not real, officer. We are going to the Vanderbilt ball. It's only a prop."

The officer snorted. "Sure you are. And I have an invitation from Queen Victoria to join her for tea."

Tyler fished the invitation from his pocket. "It's right here."

The man eyed the embossed page and then gave a sniff. "There'll be officers outside the residence tonight. Any hint of disturbance from imposters, and we'll cart you straight to jail." He wiggled his fingers. "Hand it over."

Tyler took a half step back. "On what grounds?"

"On the grounds of I said to hand it over." The officer narrowed his brown eyes.

She squeezed Tyler's arm. "Let's not have this ruin our day, right?"

He mumbled something about due cause before unstrapping the belt and holding it out.

The officer slid the curved blade from the sheath and ran his finger along the edge. "Dull as a butter knife." He pushed the blade into its sheath and returned it. "Don't take kindly to loons in this part of the city, fellow."

Tyler bristled, but she dug her fingers into his arm. "We'll be on our way. Thanks."

The officer smirked. "See that you do." With an

exaggerated swagger, he moved past them down the road.

Great. What could go wrong next?

Six

$\mathcal{B}$reathtaking. Fiona forgot her aching feet after the long walk, the rude police officer, and the manure odor as they neared the pristine residence. Cinderella's castle had nothing on the William K. Vanderbilt mansion. Designed, of course, by his enterprising wife.

"Talk about overkill." Tyler craned his neck to gawk at the peaked roof and spires rising from the majestic residence on the corner of Fifth Avenue and Fifty-Second Street.

"At least it doesn't take up the entire block," she teased.

"Might as well." He fished the crumpled invitation from his pocket and frowned at the embossed paper. "Totally out of our league."

She ignored him. They had an invitation. What more did they need to belong? After waiting for a cart to pass, she hurried across the cobbled road and up the steps to an ornate front door. She banged the brass knocker.

Tyler huffed behind her. "Don't you think we should—"

The door swung open, revealing a man with a posture and expression as stiff as his starched suit.

"May I help you?" He spoke with a British accent befitting his European features and thin nose. Which he looked down to regard the two of them.

She straightened her bearing and plucked the invitation from Tyler. "We are here for the ball."

The man's eyebrows shot toward his thinning hairline before slumping back into indifference. "There is a very strict list, as I am sure you know. Good day." He started to shut the door.

"Wait!" Tyler braced his palm on the door to keep it open. "We have an invitation from Mrs. Easley, and we must speak with her. She said to meet her here."

The man wrinkled his nose. "You do know which residence you are calling upon, do you not, sir?" Before Tyler could respond, the man clicked his tongue. "This is the Vanderbilt home. *Good day.*"

The door thudded closed.

They stared at one another before Tyler spoke. "Let's go find a phone."

"And what?" She jammed her hands on her hips. "Ask the operator to connect us to the future?"

When he pressed his lips into a line, she sighed. "I don't get it. We have an invitation."

"None of this makes sense." He pushed his fingers

through his hair. "Let's go back to the room. Look for...I don't know. A wormhole or something that takes us back to Ocean Springs."

"I don't think that's how it works."

"Then what do you suggest—"

"Excuse me? Sir?"

A masculine voice intruded behind them. A stout man in a black suit and a matching hat dipped his chin. He carried a polished wooden box with a round lens and leather handle. Antique camera? "Are they already letting in the press? I thought I was the first."

Of course! Before Tyler could say anything, she gripped his arm. "Not yet. Seems we are too early. Might be able to tour the grounds, though."

The man tipped his hat before sauntering away.

"I have an idea." She tugged her husband's elbow. "Come on."

He allowed her to pull him down the steps and onto the sidewalk, but rather than turning toward the hotel, she slipped into an alleyway between the gleaming white mansion and a brownstone.

"What are you doing?"

She glanced over her shoulder but didn't slow her pace. "It's a huge party. They've got to be delivering a bunch of stuff, right?"

"So?"

She rolled her eyes and hurried toward voices behind the house. Then she paused to peek around the corner. Sure enough, carriages crammed into the open area, and people in historical clothing darted around with flowers, linens, and…was that an entire pig?

Tyler peered over her shoulder. "You think no one is going to notice us slipping in the back door? I'm dressed like a pirate."

That was unfortunate. Why hadn't they been given other clothes instead of these costumes? "Maybe we can sneak past when no one is looking."

"Then what? How do we know if Mrs. Easley will be here before the ball starts?" His whisper gained volume, and he dropped his voice again. "The invitation didn't even say when it would begin."

"It's pretty late. Like nine or ten, I think. And it won't end until dawn." She pressed her cheek against the brick. "We could pretend to be members of the press like that other guy. They get in early to see the decorations."

"How do you know all of this?" His breath tickled her neck.

She shrugged. "Books. I've read a couple from the Gilded Age."

"That's fiction."

"Researched fiction. It's close enough." She cast him a mischievous glance. "Do you have any information from something you consider a more reliable source?"

His silence proved answer enough.

The delivery people unloaded cart after cart without a break in the steady stream. Fiona grunted. "You're right. We are going to need different clothes. We can stash these somewhere, then change back before the ball. We'll go in with everyone else. That will be less suspicious."

"And where are we going to get new clothes?" he asked as she skirted around him and strode down the alleyway.

Good question. Why hadn't the miracle package come with spending money? What were they supposed to do all afternoon without any money?

"Are you sure you didn't find anything else with that letter? Cash maybe?"

His face said "Seriously? Do you think I'm an idiot?" But his mouth replied, "Back to the room to wait, then?"

Fiona gazed up at the house. "We are only here for one night, right?"

"I hope."

She ignored the pang his words shot through her heart. "Who knows, this whole thing might be nothing more than an elaborate dream anyway."

"That seems unlikely."

"Lots of people in the Bible got dreams that were superreal. The angel came to Joseph several times in dreams to tell him about Jesus and to warn him away from Herod."

"What does that have to do with us?"

At his scowl, she turned out her palms. "I'm just saying. We don't know if we have traveled to the past for real or if it is a dream. Reality is held in the brain anyway. A dream doesn't make it any less real, if you think about it." She waved her hand. "But that's not the point. The point is at the metaphorical stroke of midnight, this carriage goes back to a pumpkin, right? And we wake up back at a quirky inn in Mississippi."

A horse clopped by, stealing his focus, but his twisted lips and furrowed brow displayed his doubts. Right. No way could this be a dream.

"Whatever the details, we are stuck here." He massaged his temple. "At least until we find Mrs. Easley and see if she can fast-track us home."

"You're missing the point." She flung out her hands. For someone so smart, how could he so often miss the simplest things? "We pretty much have a free pass."

"What does that mean?" The furrows on his forehead deepened. "You're not thinking of trying to break in, are you?"

Not necessarily. "I'm saying we can take some risks. Embrace the adventure. We'll be gone tomorrow."

"But our convictions and morals won't." He crossed his arms. "I can't believe you are talking about stealing and breaking and entering just because you might not be around tomorrow to deal with the consequences."

Heat tingled up her neck. "Is that what you think?"

A couple passing by regarded her with suspicion, so she lowered her voice.

"Why is that the first thing you assume? I meant we could take this opportunity to be bold. To take some risks. That's all."

"I'm not following."

Obviously. Even Noah would have caught on by now. "We could try, you know? Do something new? Something adventurous?"

He curled and relaxed his fingers. "Like what?"

"I don't know. Something enterprising."

Enterprising? What did she expect him to do? Waltz up to the house and demand entrance? Dressed like a pirate?

Then again… He lifted his elbow to offer her his arm. "The answer is always no until you ask, right?"

Her eyes brightened, and he remembered what it felt like when she used to look at him that way. Like he could take on the world. How long had it been since she'd stopped calling him her superman?

She took his arm with a ghost of a smile. Rather than turning them back down the alley, he led her around the main sidewalk. They walked into the courtyard with as much confidence as they could feign.

A young man, more a teen of sixteen, struggled to lift an elaborate flower arrangement from a black carriage.

"Opportunity knocks." Tyler winked at his wife and slipped away from her grasp. "Need a hand there?"

Without waiting for the answer, he tucked his palms underneath the stone pot and shifted half the weight from the boy's arms.

"Whew. Thanks, mister."

The two of them muscled the pot between them. He'd only taken two steps before Fiona swept past them, a pot of leafy foliage tucked beneath her chin. He withheld a chuckle as she sashayed ahead, green fronds sticking out past her fiery hair.

Flowers in front of their faces like some kind of movie scene, they waltzed right through the back door and into gaudiness overload.

When he'd been in middle school, a traveling tour of the Palace of Versailles had come to Jackson. All the schools had gone. They walked through a reconstruction of the hall of mirrors, gawked at the gold trim lining every surface, and rolled their eyes over the haughty furnishings.

This reminded him of that ostentatious display.

He let the boy take the lead and followed him into a two-story room. They shuffled underneath six-foot-tall paintings of stoic men to a dainty table that might not stand up to the weight of this arrangement. Nonetheless, he hefted and plopped the vase right in the center.

The boy swiped a hand across his brow. "Thanks, mister. I…"

When the kid goggled at his attire, Tyler shrugged. "Wanted to get in on the fun."

The boy blinked before deciding peculiar help was better than none at all. "Two more go in this room."

Fiona stood gaping at the decorative molding dripping from a ceiling painted with mythological scenes. On it hung a chandelier that had to have at least fifty candles on it. Wait. No. Were those candles or gaslight?

She deposited her fronds and roses on a four-person table dwarfed by the room. Then she grinned at him.

"Rest of it goes to the third floor," the boy continued. "They are turning the gymnasium up there into some kind of forest for the ball."

"Gymnasium?" Tyler scoffed. "Who needs a gymnasium in their house?"

The boy snickered. "My sisters are going to question me for hours for stepping inside the place. All the papers are supposed to be here. I even heard they are going to station policemen outside to manage the crowds."

They made their way down an opulent hallway and back out a normal-sized room lined with windows to the courtyard. He'd just stepped past the threshold when a familiar haughty voice made him pause.

"You! Miss! What are you doing?"

The stuffy butler who'd denied them entrance grabbed his wife by the arm.

Seven

Embrace the moment. Fiona pulled her shoulders back and tilted her nose in the air. She'd always despised haughty people, but now, she channeled every uppity cheerleader, self-important career maven, and holier-than-thou churchwoman she could remember into one disdainful look.

"Sir! You will unhand me immediately."

The butler's eyes flew wide, and his fingers dropped from her arm.

"Is this how Alva's staff treats her guests?" She clicked her tongue. "Then it is no wonder Caroline proved reluctant to include her in the upper echelons of society."

The use of Mrs. Vanderbilt's and Mrs. Astor's first names made the man go pale. "My apologies, Mrs.…um, that is to say."

She put a hand to her throat and shook her head. "Really. And to think I came early to give a good report to Mrs. Astor on what to expect tonight."

The tall man sputtered.

She pivoted on her heel and motioned to Tyler. "Come, my dear. I'll not be treated in this fashion."

Behind her, the flustered man still hadn't formulated a coherent reply, mumbling something that might be adjacent to an apology.

Tyler gaped at her. Then a hearty laugh bubbled from his chest. She shot him a look. He was going to ruin the whole charade! Good. Maintaining his dignity, he offered her his arm again, and they strode out of the courtyard, leaving the delivery people clamoring with questions.

They made it to the front of the house before she dissolved into laughter.

"What was that?" He leaned against the white limestone and chuckled. "That poor man looked like he might keel over."

"I figured if I dropped a few names, he might stop acting like I was a nobody."

Tyler sobered and studied her, digging deeper. "Is that how you feel?"

Leave it to him to pick this moment to start seeing straight through her teasing. She peeled her gaze from his. A well-groomed spotted horse lifted his feet high as he trundled a black carriage down the road.

"Not much glamor in wiping boogers and cleaning up spills all day. All I accomplish is tedium." The words rasped her throat. She hadn't even realized the razor-sharp truth of them until now.

"Says the woman who spends all day nurturing immortal souls. I say there's a lot of importance to that."

Guilt nudged her. "I know. I do. And I love the little monkeys. But wrangling a two- and four-year-old boy is harder than you think."

He pressed his lips together. "Because I wouldn't know."

"You're not around a lot."

"I'm home every night. A lot of guys out on the oil rig are gone weeks at a time."

Sure, someone always had it worse. Some women had to raise kids alone. But he'd promised more than that. He did come home. But either he had no energy or he was distracted by his phone. It wasn't like he was much help.

But this was supposed to be her Cinderella day, and she didn't want to spend it arguing. "I wonder if I ruffled that butler enough for him to let us back inside. We still haven't found Mrs. Easley."

"Fiona, I think we need to talk about—"

"It's fine. I get it." She peered around the corner before he could give her the line she'd heard a hundred times. "You work hard to take care of us."

With silence heavy between them, she kept her focus on the back of the house. Trying to sneak in with a delivery guy wouldn't work again. Maybe they could go as members of the press? What had happened to that photographer they saw earlier?

Firm hands wrapped around her waist and turned her around. Her breath caught at the pained look in her husband's eyes. "Tell me what I need to do to fix it. I can't quit my job."

Of course. Sometimes she just wished she felt as important as his loyalty to his family's business. "I don't know."

Hurt hardened into frustration, and his jaw ticked. "*What* would make you happy?"

Had the question not held too much emphasis on the first word she could have contained herself. Maybe the pent-up aggravation was to blame or maybe their crazy circumstances.

"How about coming home on time? Or maybe having enough consideration for the time I've spent wrangling small children while making you supper to call me and let me know you're going to be late? How about helping with bedtime routines once in a while? Or...or...maybe caring enough about your family that you want to spend what little time you have off with us instead of running to the golf course."

That struck a nerve. Their last fight had been over her apparently not wanting him to have any friends because she didn't want him to spend Saturday at the golf course and leave her home alone with the boys. Again.

Angry tears welled and spilled over her lashes. "We only get the leftovers. Your mind is always somewhere else. Yet somehow, you have time and energy to give to a bunch of guys who want to use you for your club membership. But hey, why not? Why would you want to spend your whole day dealing with temper tantrums and cleaning up poop someone dug out of their diaper to smear on the wall when you could get to go out and have fun and talk to friends? I bet that would be nice."

The anger rolled through her in waves. She shouldn't have said those things. But she'd reached some kind of breaking point.

So much for Cinderella and Prince Charming.

She spun on her heel and marched away. She was going to find that weird woman from the inn and demand to go home.

The lava from his wife's eruption sprayed over him. Dumbfounded, Tyler could only fume as she stomped away. Yes, he gave a lot to his job. Yes, he needed some downtime. But she was making him seem like a deadbeat dad who didn't do anything to care for his family. After everything he endured to give her the option to stay home with their children. Which she'd wanted. Now she wanted to spew venom and then stalk away?

He closed the distance between them in three strides and plucked his wife from the ground. She let out a startled squeak when he lifted her to his chest, securing one arm under her legs and the other behind her shoulders.

"Tyler!" Her arm wrapped around his neck, fury melting into surprise. "What are you doing?"

"You can be mad at me all you want. But you're going to do it right here." He set her down on the mansion's front entry steps. Wide eyes blinked at him. "You can take all the time you need. When you're ready to talk about this, I'll be right here."

He plopped down across from her in the middle of the sidewalk. A man in a top hat with a cane mumbled something about riffraff as he made an arc around where Tyler sat.

Fiona pursed her lips. Two more people gave him strange looks before she puffed out her cheeks. "At least sit up here on the step so you're not tripping people."

He settled next to her. The historical people went about their day while he waited for her to cool down. Had they really gone to the past? It didn't matter. If he didn't take hold of the present—loosely speaking—and be in this moment, the consequences could be long reaching for his family.

He sent up a prayer for God to help him with his

tongue. Then he grasped his wife's trembling hand. At least she didn't pull away. "Remember that marriage seminar they had at church?"

"Yeah."

"They had that communication drill. We should try it."

She wrinkled her nose. "That thing? It's so silly. You say something, and then all I do is repeat it back to you. That's pointless."

"I don't think that's the idea. Let's try it." When she didn't respond, he took the first step. "What I heard you say is that I am a deadbeat dad who has left raising our children up to you and that I must not love my family."

Furrows formed on her brow. "That's not what I said."

"That's what I hear you mean."

They sat in silence until she said, "When you tell me how important your job is, all I hear is that it's more important than me."

"Nothing is more important than you and the boys. That's why I put up with everything I have to deal with at work—so I can provide for you."

Her eyes glistened. "But if you are so busy providing that you aren't ever there for us, what's the point? Don't you know I'd rather have you than the things you provide?"

The statement knifed deep into a tender place. Did he know that? Or had he somehow equated his worth to his wife with what he could give her? "Thank you, love."

"I know you work hard for us. I really do. But I feel lonely and neglected while you're doing it." Gentle tears snaked down her cheeks. "I don't know how to fix it. To fix us."

He wrapped his arm around her and pulled her to him.

A man will give himself up for his wife, just as Christ did for the church.

But what did that mean? How much more could he give up for her when he already gave every ounce of himself to give her everything she wanted?

The moment stretched long as they sat on the opulent mansion's front step, lost in time and lost to one another.

Eight

"What are you two doing out here?" A bubbly feminine voice drew Fiona's gaze up from the sidewalk.

Tyler popped to his feet. "Mrs. Easley. There you are. We've been looking for you. Where are we? What's happened? Are our boys okay? How do we get out of here?"

The older woman placed a hand on the hip of a tailored pale-yellow walking dress and clicked her tongue. "My, but aren't you in a hurry? So many questions all at once. Which would you like me to answer first?"

Fiona stepped onto the sidewalk. "*Are* we in the past?"

"Certainly." Mrs. Easley beamed. "Isn't it lovely? It's been ages since I've seen New York's forgotten splendor." She peered down the road to something beyond their view. "There was a time when..." She cleared sudden emotion from her voice. "Never mind that. There I go, reminiscing about things having nothing to do with helping you with your adventure."

The statement opened up a host of other questions about how often Mrs. Easley had gone to the past and how old she must really be, but Fiona didn't get the chance to chase those curious rabbits.

"*Why* are we in the past?" Tyler jabbed a finger in the air. "And how do we get out of it?"

Mrs. Easley adjusted her feathered hat. "The question that is truly bothering you is if your children are safe and if you will return to them. Correct?"

Fiona and Tyler both nodded.

"While I generally don't give such information to my guests"—Mrs. Easley waved a gloved hand— "messes with the process, you see. In this instance, I have been given leeway to ease your minds else you might never find what you were sent here to discover."

"And what is that?"

The woman lifted an eyebrow at Tyler until he pressed his lips into a line. "As I told you before, you won't be gone for longer than you planned to be. Any arrangements you made for childcare will not be hindered or altered in any way. You will return to The Depot and depart for your residence at your scheduled time."

Fiona let out a relieved breath. "Thank goodness for that."

"Yes, but that doesn't explain why we are here."

"You are here because you need to be, young man. That's the way it works. I won't claim to understand everything about how the Conductor goes about his business, but I'm certain of one thing. Everyone who goes somewhere on a trip does so because it's what's best for them."

"So not everyone who stays at your inn gets sent to the Gilded Age in New York?" How interesting.

"Of course not, dear." Chuckling, Mrs. Easley patted Fiona's hand. "Maddie enjoyed her time in the fifties, and that one couple had the grandest adventure on the Oregon Trail."

Fiona worked her mouth, but words didn't come.

"Assuming any of that is true, how do we get back home?" Tyler asked.

One finger poised to her lips, Mrs. Easley regarded him. "Only the Conductor decides when the trip is completed."

"But you said we would be back in time to go home to our boys."

"And you shall."

The muscle in the side of his jaw twitched. "And does that mean we are stuck here until then?"

"Stuck?" The lady tilted her head. "Is that how you view the miracle you've been granted? Hmm. Perhaps your lack of trust is one of the reasons you're here. Along with your deep need for control. That's the real reason behind your question, isn't it? You want to know *how* to go back so you get to be the one who determines *when* you go back."

Tyler shifted under her penetrating gaze. When was the last time he'd looked so uncomfortable?

Best to give him a moment to regroup. "So, like Cinderella, we have been given one special night to enjoy the ball. Then it's back to life as usual."

"That is my understanding, yes." Mrs. Easley smiled and spread out her hands. "Beautiful, isn't it?"

"Yes, it is." Fiona tipped her head in thanks, then motioned toward the door. "Only problem is they don't want to let us in."

"Of course not, child. You are still five hours early. The ball won't start until ten." She tapped a finger on her chin. "And I imagine you strike them as rather odd, as ordinary ladies and gentlemen do not go about town in costume-ball attire."

Fiona spluttered. They wore the only attire *she* had given them! Tyler stepped in before she had the chance to point that out.

"And what are we supposed to do until then?" He pinned his arms over his pirate's shirt.

"Surely I don't need to tell you how to spend a romantic getaway with your wife, do I?" A sideways smile plucked Mrs. Easley's rosy lips.

Tyler's face reddened.

A nervous giggle bubbled free, and Fiona cleared her throat. "Okay, so we have the day to ourselves, and about ten tonight, they will let us into the ball, right?" At Mrs. Easley's nod, Fiona probed, "And then once the ball is over, we go home."

The woman's somewhat ageless features glowed. "Yes, dear. That's what I keep telling you."

Right. They had been over this a few times. Though in Fiona's defense, crazy situations required more clarity. "Is there any way to get more clothes?"

Mrs. Easley's lips compressed. "What for?"

"You said it's strange to go around in these costumes, right?" Gesturing to those passing by, Fiona added a leading quality to the question.

"Does it matter what people think? You're here for you, not them."

Not the answer she'd been expecting.

"What about money?" Tyler asked. "How can I take her to eat or anything without money?"

"My dear boy, for someone so smart, you're starting to make me wonder about you." She tittered, belying her words, then jutted her chin toward him. "Didn't you check your wallet?"

"Wallet? I don't have a…" He grunted as he pulled a billfold from his jacket pocket.

The impish woman bounced on her toes.

Fiona leaned close to inspect the one-dollar bill he displayed. George Washington still graced the face. But a picture of a bunch of people demarked the left corner, and a red seal stamped the other side. Tyler counted out nine more dollars and one five-dollar bill.

"Thank you. But I'm not sure what we'll be able to find in New York City for fifteen dollars."

Her poor husband must be too flustered to think about the rate of inflation from 1883 to their own time.

"I think," Fiona supplied, "that one dollar here should be about twenty to us." She linked her gaze to his. "Right?"

The corners of Mrs. Easley's eyes creased. "Enough for a nice dinner and perhaps a trinket, yes?"

"This is crazy." Tyler crinkled the money, then whispered. "You see that, right? It's crazy."

Fiona matched his whisper. "Crazy or not, it's our reality. At least we found out we have some money. We should thank her."

He lifted his head and dropped the wallet. "Where'd she go?"

Fiona plucked the leather billfold from the ground. She scanned the street, but didn't see Mrs. Easley's bustled yellow gown.

People strolled along. Horses clopped down the street pulling carriages. But no sign of a feisty older woman with a mischievous bent. Surely she couldn't have disappeared that fast.

"Think she'll come back?" Tyler asked.

Who could say? "That woman is a mystery."

"What else do you expect? Crazy woman for a crazy day."

"That's like the eighth time you've said crazy."

"It's fitting." He stuffed the billfold into his pocket. "What now?"

Now he was supposed to sweep her off her feet. In a metaphorically romantic way, not like what he'd done earlier to keep her from storming off. She was still mad at him, for the record. There was just too much going on to deal with that right now.

"Weird fairy godmother, check." Fiona mumbled. "Fancy ball gown." She swept a hand over her shimmering Regency fabric. "Sort of." She pointed at a single horse-drawn carriage consisting of two wheels and a two-person seat with windowed sides and an open front. A driver with a whip perched on a seat at the rear of the cab holding reins that stretched over the top of the passenger seat and down to the horse. "Next is the pumpkin, I suppose."

Tyler followed her line of sight. "Is that the historical version of a taxi?"

"I think so. Guess we'll have to ask."

They hurried past two brownstone townhouses and neared the "taxi."

"Excuse me?" Tyler gained the man's attention. "Is this a taxi?"

The young man, no more than eighteen years old, tipped his hat back. "What, sir?"

"He means is this conveyance for hire," Fiona supplied.

The boy took in their costumes before giving a slow nod. "It is. Fare's forty cents per mile for the two of ye."

Tyler clasped Fiona's hand. "I'll give you a dollar for a tour of the city and then taking us to the best restaurant around."

The boy tilted his hat back over his blond hair. "Best restaurant, sir? That would be Delmonico's. But I'm not sure if they'll let you in dressed like that."

Tyler scoffed. "You mean my costume for tonight's Vanderbilt ball?"

Fiona lifted her hand to cover her mouth. Maybe there was hope to uncover his inner Prince Charming.

The men agreed on the fee, and then Tyler helped her up the foot step to settle onto the maroon leather seat. She arranged her skirts like she thought a lady might. "I'd forgotten about Delmonico's. That's one of the most famous restaurants in New York history."

He swung onto the seat beside her and plopped down. "Something else you learned from one of your books?"

"Yep. I read a couple about the New York 400 and the parties they threw. Women in the books were always talking about Delmonico's."

"But that's fiction."

"So? Doesn't mean the restaurant isn't real."

The driver tapped the reins across the back of the black horse, and the carriage rolled into the street traffic. They traveled down Fifth Avenue and a line of mansions.

When they neared a stately brownstone residence, Tyler waved toward it. "I think that's where the Empire State building is supposed to be."

"Really?"

He lifted one shoulder. "I think so. But I don't know much about all this history. Bet if we were to come back in our time this entire street wouldn't be anything but neon lights and stores."

"Well, it is Fifth Avenue."

They sat back to enjoy the ride and gawk at the passing architecture. The buildings were so different from theirs in modern times. Molding and detail reigned where steel and glass would later take the throne.

People strolled along the paved streets and sidewalks like a giant cast from a high-budget movie. Amazing.

"Can you imagine dressing like that every day?" Tyler nodded toward a man in a tall hat.

"Better than ragged jeans and yoga pants like back home." She ogled a woman in a sumptuous pink dress. "So much more class and style."

Beyond the lady stood a building with striped awnings and scrolled metal railings along the balconies. Everything about the place, from the design to the people entering and exiting, spoke of a more sophisticated era.

What must it have been like to live in this time?

The horse's hooves clicked over the pavers in a steady rhythm. It would have been nice to know something about the buildings, but the sights filled her senses to the brim. After another thirty minutes, the cab stopped before an impressive structure.

The driver dismounted and stood by the horse's back legs. "Here we are, sir—Delmonico's. Restaurant has a ballroom on the second floor, I hear. Though they might not be doing anything tonight seeing as how the Vanderbilts are having their home-welcoming ball."

"That's where we will be." Tyler swung down from the carriage. "Would you mind returning here at nine thirty to pick us up?"

The boy dismounted. "Of course, sir. It would be my pleasure." He tipped his hat and accepted the dollar bill Tyler handed him. "If you don't mind my asking, have you been here before?"

"No. Have you?"

The boy chortled as if Tyler had said something outrageous. "I heard some folks last week talking about a dish called the Lobster Newburg. Said it was awful good."

"Thanks," Tyler replied. "Hey, what's your name?"

The boy paused with one hand on the carriage. "Sam Florence, sir."

"Thanks, Sam. We're Tyler and Fiona Robinson. I appreciate the recommendation. We'll see you again at nine thirty."

"Yes, sir. I'll be here." He tipped his chin and swung back up into the rear of the vehicle.

The carriage rumbled away as Tyler offered his arm. Fiona looped her hand through his elbow and then stepped inside another stunning view of the past.

Nine

$\mathcal{O}$f all the nerve. Tyler did his best to maintain a pleasant expression for the man at the host station. "No, we don't have a reservation, and no, we haven't eaten here before."

"Then I'm sorry, sir, but we cannot—"

"And here I thought to treat my wife to what I've heard is the best restaurant in the city before we attend the Vanderbilt ball. I will simply have to tell my friends about the poor service we discovered at Delmonico's. I won't be ordering any catering from here. That's for sure."

The man's face paled with each sentence until he held up a hand. "The ball, sir?"

"Of course the ball. Why else would I be dressed like this?" He gestured to his pirate's costume and then leaned closer to the stand the man fortified himself behind. "My wife's historical costume was specially made. We did think wearing them now might give the people an early peek but..." He spread his hands.

"Oh yes. I'm sorry, sir." He glanced past Tyler to Fiona, who stood by the doorway looking regal. "Let me check. We may have a table available in one of our more private areas."

The man scuttled off.

Fiona came to stand beside him. "Were you able to get a table without a reservation? I know it's 1883 and all, but this is still New York."

"He's going to find us one in a special section." Pride tipped his words. He had been rather clever, using Fiona's tactic of name-dropping and aristocratic talk.

"I hope that doesn't mean something tucked up by the kitchen where they put the undesirables."

His fingers twitched. Didn't she trust him to do anything right?

The mustached man in his pressed black suit returned. "If you will follow me, please, sir, ma'am." He gave a tiny bow before turning on his heel.

Past the foyer, they entered an extravagant chamber with white linens, crystal, and china-topped immaculate tables. People in their weirdly fancy historical clothes chatted and sipped wine underneath twinkling chandeliers.

One woman with a pinched face so white she must have smothered it in rice powder noticed them and whispered to the younger brunette next to her. Within seconds, one table then the next all gawked.

Not that he cared.

But his tense shoulders still loosened when they entered a smaller section where the spread-out tables offered discreet privacy amid the potted plants creating the illusion of a garden area. The host took them to the rear and past a leafy fern.

"Will this do, sir? It is one of Mr. William Vanderbilt's preferred tables."

Tyler did his best not to look impressed. "This will do. Thank you."

The man offered another slight bow and left them.

Fiona grabbed her chair, but he hurried to take it from her. "I've got you."

He pulled the chair, and a glimmer of delight lit her features before she settled and scooted closer. He sat across from her and placed his hands in his lap, feeling strangely awkward.

The waiter, a man similar to the host in manner and dress, arrived with two menus. Tyler reached for his, and his heartbeat stuttered at the prices of sixty-five and seventy-five. Er—wait, those were cents. Right. He let out a low whistle. Steak cost a dollar. No lobster, though. And why did half of these words look like French?

"I was too hard on you earlier. I'm sorry." Fiona's stiff words landed between them after the waiter walked away.

He set down the menu. "How long have you been feeling that way?"

One puffy-sleeved shoulder lifted. "A lot of times I feel like a single mom."

His back stiffened as the words knifed through him. "How's that fair, Fiona? I work my tail off trying to give you everything you want, and you say I'm not doing anything?"

"I didn't say that."

"It's what I heard."

She puffed out a breath. "Well, what I hear when you ask me to go play golf with your friends is that the sixty hours a week you were already gone wasn't enough and you need to find somewhere to be on Saturday too so you can escape. But I get it—I do. It must be nice to have other adults to spend time with."

Some of her friendships had fizzled out when they'd had children before most of their friends, but she hadn't said much about it. "I don't want to fight with you. We are supposed to be having a nice evening."

"You're right." She hoisted her menu between them.

"How do we fix this, love? I don't know what else to do."

When she lowered her menu, tears simmered. "I don't know."

The waiter returned and stood at their table, hands folded behind his back. "Have you made your selections, sir?"

"I don't see the lobster. I was told it was not to be

missed."

The man blinked. "As this is May, sir, and as the season will not start until June, we don't yet have lobster available." He pointed to the menu. "Might I suggest our mignon de filet with champignons frais?"

May? They'd left home in March. Tyler shook the thought free and focused on the rest of what the man had said. "Mignon de filet" sounded like filet mignon. Should be safe enough. "That's fine." He searched for anything in English. "Bring the asparagus and two tomato salads as well."

"Very good, sir."

He looked back at the hors d'oeuvres, which even he knew meant appetizers. Sardines? Weird. "The olives, as well."

"Dénoyauté ou farci?"

He had no idea what that meant. Why didn't the guy use English? Looked like there were two cheap options for olives, though. "Both." Something else caught his eye. "And the caviar."

The waiter's otherwise droll expression brightened. "Very good, sir." He dipped a shallow bow and left with their menus.

"Caviar?" Fiona lifted her eyebrows.

"Figured this is the cheapest we'll ever find it. Might be a good time to try it."

She chuckled. "What all did you order for us? He didn't even ask me."

"Probably custom in this time. I got us both a filet mignon, I think. Then some asparagus in hollandaise sauce. Olives for the appetizer, but I have no idea what kind or what he was talking about."

Minutes later, the waiter reappeared with a bowl of pitted black olives and a tray of green stuffed with garlic, peppers, and maybe almonds.

She plucked one and sampled it. "Not bad."

Next came two miniature glass bowls of black pellets nestled in crushed ice, each accompanied by three triangular crackers. Must be the caviar.

When the waiter retreated, Fiona wrinkled her nose. "You sure you want to eat this?"

"It's supposed to be one of the world's greatest delicacies." He winked. "Adventure, remember?"

That sparked a smile, and she dipped out a heaping spoonful. She lifted it toward him. "To adventure."

He matched her scoop and raised his spoon in a mock toast. "To adventure."

Together, they took a bite.

The taste of salt water settled on his tongue. He pushed the pellets around his mouth and tried not to grimace. The flavor shifted to…butter? Maybe he was supposed to chew it to get past the salty-fish taste. He shouldn't have gotten such a big spoonful. He chewed, and the texture turned to unappealing mush.

His throat constricted, resisting the thought of swallowing. But he couldn't spit it out.

Across from him, Fiona's eyes watered. Her mouth didn't move. She blinked at him and shook her head.

The waiter chose that moment to return to the table. "How are you enjoying the caviar, sir?"

He started to sweat. It tasted like salt and fish and butter and refused to go down his throat. He forced a smile and gave the man a thumbs-up.

The waiter frowned. "Is something the matter, sir?"

His stomach heaved. He couldn't choke. Wouldn't. With sheer determination, he forced his muscles to swallow.

And gaged.

The slime slid down his throat. He gripped the table.

"Sir, do you need assistance?"

Fiona bolted from her seat, knocking the chair over in her haste. Her cheeks puffed out, and her eyes watered. The world slid into slow motion. She pitched forward. The tablecloth stretched as her body pulled against it.

The waiter yelped.

Tyler reached for his wife.

Too late.

She stumbled forward, grabbed the waiter, and puked caviar all down the front of his shirt.

She'd never been so mortified in her life. Fiona leaned over the powder room sink. She splashed cold water on her face, thankful one of the most prestigious businesses in New York City had indoor plumbing. Sure, the toilet looked like some kind of wooden-box thing, and the water pressure in the sink was pitiful. But it *was* a bathroom.

She might die if she'd had to find an outhouse. She might as well die of embarrassment now. After she'd spewed the fishy balls of slime all over the waiter, he'd stoically directed her up the stairs to the second floor and to the women's room on the left.

Drying her face with a terry cloth, she studied her reflection in the wavy mirror. She looked a wreck. No hope of freshening her makeup, either. Bet Cinderella never had to worry about choking on caviar.

The door behind her opened, and a woman in a flouncy dress entered. Ruffles fell from her waist to the floor, and the train draped over her bustle trailed her into the bathroom. Long white sleeves and burgundy bows topped a torso with an impossibly tiny waist.

"Oh." The brunette pursed her rosy lips. "Are you quite all right, ma'am?"

Ma'am. Way to make her feel over a century. This wasn't the South, so she couldn't even pretend the title was given out of custom. It was something one said to their elders. The perfectly poised twentysomething moved farther into the room, concern on her smooth features.

"I'm old!" The words squeaked out before she could stop herself, and she slumped against the counter. "And I puked caviar all over the waiter!"

The young woman placed a comforting gloved palm on Fiona's arm. "There now. It can't be that bad." Her mouth lifted in a gentle curve. "I never did much care for caviar myself. Though my husband believes it to be the best of delicacies."

Facing the mirror, Fiona dabbed her eyes and frowned at the dark smudges underneath. "I'm mortified."

"I once got my bustle caught on a stray nail on Mrs. Hamilton's settee. It ripped my dress open. And of course, I could never tell anyone Mrs. Hamilton's furniture was in such disarray. I was left to suffer the humiliation of every lady at tea thinking I had gone out in public in such disgrace."

Laughter bubbled from Fiona's center. "So what did you do?"

The girl beamed. "I held my chin high, feigned a headache, and went home with my petticoat showing."

A peek of a petticoat sounded far better than public vomiting, but she appreciated the attempt. "I'm Fiona."

The other woman blinked in surprise. "Mrs. Betty Wainsworth. But you may call me Betty as I see we are already fast friends."

Oh, right. How had she forgotten about the first-name-formality thing? "Sorry. Mrs. Fiona Robinson. I'm afraid I've forgotten myself."

"That's quite all right." Betty waved away the misstep. "Forgive my forwardness—it is a quality Mother always said would bring me trouble—but I simply must know. Why are you dressed in this manner?"

Fiona pinched one of her puffed sleeves. "It's a costume for the ball. It's supposed to be from the Regency era, I think."

"You're invited to the ball?" Betty fanned her face. "We were planning on watching as they entered. Discreetly, of course. George wouldn't dream of us standing out on the street gawking." Her lips tipped. "Though he did agree there was no harm in passing by the Vanderbilt residence on our way home after dinner."

She couldn't help but like Betty. "Well done, Mrs. Wainsworth."

Betty inclined her head with a triumphant smile.

"I don't even know if I should go." Fiona sighed. "My costume is rumpled, my husband is a pirate, and the butler at the door was terrible."

The younger woman brightened despite Fiona's illogical ramble. "Your dress can be righted, and a lady can always ignore a sour servant. An event such as this is not to be missed."

"It does go down in history as one of the grandest and most expensive nights on record."

"I've no doubt that it will." Betty clapped. "Now, let's see. Some powder, yes. Then we'll fix your pins here and here."

Ten minutes later, Betty had Fiona looking like a new woman.

She swept her new friend into a hug. "Thank you, Betty. Your kindness has saved me a mountain of embarrassment."

Betty patted her back. "Think nothing of it. We are always to look for opportunities to serve, yes? Jesus washed feet. The least I can do is dab powder to better another lady's evening."

Fiona left the ladies' room with her chin held high and Betty's words cycling through her heart.

She'd let resentment grow and hunted flaws when she should have been seeking to be kind. She'd been so focused on how her husband wasn't loving her the way she wanted that she'd forgotten simple things like finding ways to make him smile.

Help me, Lord, to learn to wash some feet.

Well, metaphorically speaking, of course.

Ten

Tyler held in a smirk when the waiter, dressed in a clean shirt, set their bill on the table and moved two steps back as though he feared another episode.

Fiona tapped her spoon on the edge of her gold-trimmed glass bowl. "The homemade vanilla-bean ice cream was fabulous."

The waiter pursed his lips with a dubious glance at her, dipped into a slight bow, and then hurried away.

After the caviar disaster, Fiona had spent twenty minutes in the bathroom, during which time the waiter had peeked out at Tyler from behind the palm fronds. Repeatedly. He didn't bring their steaks until she returned.

Tyler had expected her to be flustered at the least and sour at worst, but she'd returned with a bubbly description of nineteenth-century bathrooms. They'd enjoyed their steaks while having a good laugh over the absurdity of their day. It almost seemed like a different woman returned from the bathroom. He'd wanted to ask what had so shifted her mood, but he didn't want to spoil the good thing they had going.

He plucked the handwritten tally from the table. "Let's see. One fancy historical dinner complete with who-in-the-world-knows-why-it's-a-delicacy caviar and dessert for…" He cleared his throat, earning a grin from his wife. "Five dollars and eighty-five cents. We'll leave the waiter a generous tip for his trouble and round things out at a grand total of eight dollars."

Fiona laughed as he plucked the bills from his wallet. "I could get used to dinners like this."

"Maybe Mrs. Easley has a dinner-only pass for next time." He winked at her as the waiter returned and he handed over the ticket and money. "No change necessary."

The waiter's eyebrows rose. "Thank you, sir. I hope you and the misses had a pleasant evening."

"We did, though I believe we shall not sample fish eggs again." His attempt at humor was lost on the man.

The waiter grimaced. "Likely for the best, sir. Have a good evening."

After he retreated, Fiona rose and patted her stomach. "Goodness, I'm stuffed."

Tyler offered his arm and led her out of the restaurant. Many of the patrons remained the same, lingering over their plates as their gazes followed the strange people in their midst. If only they knew the truth about the woman in a Jane Austen dress and her pirate husband. What would they think about time travelers?

Whoa. Had he ever seen a man from the future without knowing it? No. Too weird to think about.

A waiter with a tray stepped into Tyler's path, and he moved to the side to allow the man to pass. As he did, a woman nearby let out a high-pitched yelp. Tyler's head swung at the sound. Oh, shoot. He'd forgotten the sword hanging at his side poked out past the long tails on his jacket. It must have brushed against the prim lady and startled her. Just then, her body pitched forward, spilling her glass of wine all over the table. Men rose from their seats with startled exclamations.

"I'm sorry, ma'am. I forgot how long this thing was."

The woman reared back like she thought he intended to stab her, and Tyler held out a palm in surrender.

"Just part of the costume, ladies and gentlemen."

Their waiter from earlier scurried through the room with impressive speed. Two others followed, cleaning rags and new tablecloth in hand.

"My apologies." Tyler backed away from the table, careful of the sheathed blade.

They hurried outside as angry voices rose. *Man.* That had to be the most accident-laden dinner of their lives.

Fiona chuckled as they burst out into the cool night air. Almost a giggle, actually, which was something he hadn't heard from his wife in a while.

"Well, we did want an adventure."

Adventure, disaster. However she wanted to look at it. He bent at the waist in a dramatic bow. "As you wish, my lady."

People eyed them as they passed, but he didn't care. How long had it been since they'd had so much fun together? This ball might be a blast after all. He checked his arm. "So weird not having a watch."

"I don't know what time we got here, but it doesn't feel like it should be nine thirty yet."

"Care for a little people watching?" He gestured toward where carriages with lights on their sides rumbled down the road. They'd always loved doing that when they were two broke newlyweds.

"Too bad we don't have an air cannon. Remember that?"

How could he forget? "That was the best part of our trip to Universal Studios. We had more fun sniping people with puffs of air and watching them wonder where it came from than we did on any of the rides."

"Oh man. Can't you just see knocking off one of those big top hats from a guy's head?"

Tyler barked a laugh. "That would be hilarious."

They reminisced and pointed out interesting outfits while they waited for Sam to return with the carriage. The crowd thickened as the night grew later. Lamplight cast yellow halos over men in suits and women in gowns ready for a formal night on the town.

Tyler nodded toward one lavish couple. "They say New York is the city that never sleeps. Guess that's true even in the eighteen hundreds. I wonder where they're going?"

"Wow. Look at the really tall hat that man is sporting, and her green dress sure is pretty. All those pearl buttons and that tailored shimmering silk. You think they all went home and changed for an evening out?"

"Women get gussied up for a night out no matter the year."

"Yeah, good point." She ran a hand over her embroidered dress.

They really should go out on more dates. For now, he dipped into another bow, hoping to entice a giggle. "I'm looking forward to escorting you to the ball."

Fiona chirped an airy laugh and attempted a deep curtsy, but either she swept her foot too far behind her or her shoe got tangled in her dress because she lost her balance and stumbled.

"Easy, Cinderella." He grabbed her waist. "You can't break an ankle before we get there. How would I be able to dance with you?"

She leaned into him. "How long has it been since we danced?"

"Are we counting that time we went to a club in college?"

"No." She made a sour face. "Let's forget we ever did that."

"Then I guess since our wedding." Had it been so long since he'd danced with his wife? She loved dancing. It had been one of the many things they'd forgotten in the busyness of life.

No time like the present. He took her hand and twirled her on the sidewalk. "We'll make up for it. We'll dance until your toes fall off."

"That might make walking home a bit awkward." She pivoted around him in a swish of silk.

"Then I'll carry you." He tipped her backward. "That's dashing and debonair, right?"

"The most." Her eyes sparkled.

She was beautiful. She deserved romance and glamor and—

"Don't move." A gruff voice cut into their banter.

Tyler's blood ran cold as the tip of something hard pressed into his side.

Eleven

The terror in Fiona's eyes flushed heat through Tyler's core. Her face paled as her mouth worked, but no words came.

The gruff man poked the pistol harder into his side.

Fiona clung to him, fingers turning to claws.

"Hand over your money, dandy boy, and nobody gets hurt."

Fire scorched Tyler's center and down through his fingers. He released his wife. When she eased back a step, he gestured with his chin, hoping she would understand his unspoken directions.

Move back, love. A little more.

And she did. As soon as she was out of the way, he pivoted and grabbed the man's wrist, causing a startled curse. A hard circular twist and the thug's fingers opened. A pistol clattered to the ground. Heart pounding, he tightened his grip as the man snarled.

"I'm going to kill you for that, you—"

A shrill whistle cut through the air, and the man's

flat face went rigid. He tugged, but Tyler held firm. He splayed his thumb to catch the side of the man's hand, making the joint lock. Then he stepped through as he'd been taught, forcing the larger man into an arm bar.

The whistle sounded again, and three police officers surrounded them.

"What's happening here?" an authoritative voice demanded.

Tyler jutted his chin at the bent-over mugger, just now noticing the ragged state of his clothing. "He tried to rob us. His gun is right there."

A second burly officer scooped the weapon from the ground while the first one fished out a pair of handcuffs.

The officer took the other man from Tyler's grip and turned the perpetrator toward the light. "Max. Didn't I tell you what would happen if I caught you in this district again?"

The man he'd called Max grunted in reply.

"Tyler! I was terrified." Fiona rushed to his side.

He tucked an arm around her. "Are you all right?"

"I'm fine. Are you?"

He nodded. "Who knew that year of hapkido classes we took for fun would come in so handy?"

Two of the officers hauled away the would-be robber while the oldest of the trio stayed behind. His lids narrowed at Tyler's outfit.

Before he could ask, Tyler said, "We were having

dinner before we attend the Vanderbilt ball. That man attempted to rob me, but I was able to make him drop his weapon. I'm thankful you showed up when you did."

The officer's gaze drifted over to Fiona. "Heard it was a costume ball. We are down here to keep the crowds under control tonight. Lots of folks wanting to glimpse the elite in their finery."

His expression said he didn't believe they fit into that category. "Will you be pressing charges, then?"

And risk spending the evening at a police station? "I'm just glad he didn't try to shoot first, then take my money."

"Very well." The officer snorted. "Keep your eyes out for scoundrels hoping to prey on the people here for the event." He strode to where the other men were loading the mugger into the back of a boxy carriage with barred windows.

"Whew." Fiona fiddled with her dress collar. "I'm all for adventure, but not like that. Are you sure you're okay?"

He pulled her close. "I'm fine."

Her pert lips curved. "You were pretty awesome, you know. Disarming him like that."

Lucky. Or blessed, more likely. That could have gone a lot worse. Still, it sure was nice having her look at him like a hero. For the first time in a long while. He kissed her forehead. "Let's get to the ball and off the street."

"But what about Sam?"

Oh, right, their driver. He glanced both ways down the street, not seeing the carriage. "I guess he's not coming back." Either way, he didn't want to keep standing here. There had to be another cab available.

Even as he started looking for another coach, the black carriage rolled to a stop in front of them, and the kid from earlier hopped down from the rear. "Evening, Mr. and Mrs. Robinson. Did you enjoy your dinner?"

"We did," Tyler answered. "Thank you for the recommendation."

The boy tipped his hat, curious gaze snagging on the policemen and their jail carriage. Tyler helped Fiona onto the seat and then settled next to her before he let some of the stiffness out of his spine. Too bad there were only side windows and nothing on the front. It was getting chilly. Fiona must be freezing.

"Do you want my jacket?"

She shook her head. "Not right now. I'm overheated from the scare."

Adrenaline still pumped through his veins, making him jittery. He bounced his knee. How long could it take to merge into horse traffic?

Fiona placed a hand on his leg and leaned in closer. "You were very brave. I'm so proud of you."

Her words released something in him he didn't realize had been bound. He took her hand and kissed her knuckles. "Thanks, love."

Hand in hand, they rode in silence over the bumpy street. The further they moved from the restaurant, the more he relaxed. It could have been so much worse. Disastrous, even. If they'd ended up injured—or worse—what would have happened to the boys?

The carriage stopped moments later, and she eyed the shadowy road ahead. "Looks like bumper-to-bumper traffic."

"Or maybe muzzle to tail?"

She pressed her lips against a laugh. "Guess so."

People gathered on the streets in droves now. They lined the sidewalks like it was the Thanksgiving parade.

Crazy. "All this to watch some rich people in costumes?"

Fiona practically pressed her nose to the glass. "It's been the talk of the city for weeks now. They're all curious. Back in this time, costume parties weren't common."

"You're really into this, huh?"

She shrugged, but she didn't pull her focus from the street.

He still couldn't believe they'd traveled to the past. This was more likely some ultra-weird dream. He tried not to think on it too much, or it made his brain hurt. But dream or not, he hadn't seen her look this alive in months. The realization landed hard.

"I'm sorry things have been so hectic with us taking up managing the company."

She turned, and the war between hope and hesitation in her gaze poked him.

"When we get home, I'm going to schedule a regular date night."

That enchanting sparkle returned. "You mean it?"

His chest pinched. "We'll get a babysitter, and I'll leave my phone at home. If anyone has an emergency, they can call you."

She threw her arms around his neck and pressed into him. He breathed in the honeyed scent of her body wash.

"I'll do better, love." He whispered next to her ear. "I promise."

"Thank you for making time for us. It means a lot." She ran her tongue along her lips. "And I'll try to do better too. I know you have a lot on your plate. I've been so focused on the negatives that I've let myself lose sight of all the good things we have."

Rather than answering her, he tipped her chin and found the sweetness of her lips. She melted into him. He deepened the kiss, letting his hands roam her back and up into the softness of her hair. He lost himself in her, enjoying the passion of his bride.

A knock sounded at the window.

Startled, he released Fiona when she squeaked. Through the glass, Sam's wide eyes stared over red cheeks.

Maybe he should tell the kid to get back up in that

driver's seat and take them to their room at the hotel. So tempting. But that wouldn't be fair to Fiona. She needed to have her night out.

Sam shifted his feet. "I'm sorry. I didn't, I mean…" He tugged on his collar. "Sorry to interrupt, sir."

Tyler adjusted the collar on his pirate jacket and nodded for the kid to continue. He must have interrupted for a reason.

"We, um, we're here, sir. Close as I can get, anyway. Rest of them came in special carriages, looks like. Can't get no closer."

Though they were still in the middle of the road, Tyler stepped out of the carriage while Fiona righted herself. He fished two dollar bills from his wallet and held them out to Sam. "Thanks for the ride."

The boy's eyes rounded further, though Tyler wouldn't have thought that possible. "Um, thank you, sir. You need me to come back again?"

"This should be over at dawn. Think you can be here then to take us back to the Fifth Avenue Hotel?"

"Yes, sir."

"We might decide we want to go back to our room early, though." The best explanation he could muster for if Mrs. Easley time-warped them away before they left the mansion. "So I'm sorry if we aren't here when you come." There wasn't any way to call the kid, so the caveat was the best he could do.

He started to help Fiona out but paused at the high-pitched response.

"I…" The boy cleared his throat. "I understand, sir."

Red crept up the boy's collar and spilled more color into his cheeks.

Tyler bit back a snicker at the kid's understanding of his explanation and extended his hand for Fiona to step down.

She joined him on the sidewalk and cast a glance at Sam. "What was that all about?"

"Just letting him know to pick us up in the morning."

Sam leapt into the driver's seat and urged the horse ahead. He didn't get farther than a few dozen feet before he hit traffic again. Only then did Tyler realize the line of carriages. Down the line, one stopped before the entrance. A man in a tailored green uniform sprang from his perch and opened a gilded door.

"Oh my word." Fiona put her fingers to her lips as the woman inside stepped down.

No words at all for him. His mouth had to be catching flies. He could only stare at the craziest outfit he'd ever seen.

Twelve

She had to give the woman credit. It must be difficult to remain that poised with a stuffed cat on her head. Not a cute and cuddly toy a child might wag around, either. No, that was a taxidermied top half of a once-living creature.

Fiona could only stare.

The woman wore a gorgeous white gown overlaid with delicate lace. The sleeves draped over her shoulders. Had that been the extent of the outfit, Fiona might have still considered her elegant. Yet a blue ribbon choker like something girls from middle school found cute collared her neck with the word *puss* in silver letters. Underneath the letters hung a delicate bell.

And the entire bottom of the dress consisted of white cats' tails. Real cat tails.

The worst of it, of course, was the angry white cat that appeared to rise from the grave of her curled hair. Whoever had stuffed the pitiful thing had done a poor job of it. The ears crinkled in strange directions, and the eyes narrowed in a deranged scowl. Fiona shuddered. Had that been the woman's pet?

"Best steer clear of that one," Tyler said in her ear.

She agreed. Nothing shouted "Crazy Woman!" more than wearing a dead animal as a hat.

The bizarre woman and several other costumed people headed toward the mansion. The crowd swelled in the street as women perched on their toes to see the outlandish costumes. Fiona and Tyler followed a woman in an orange-and-black striped bee dress, complete with fabricated wings.

After they waited at least ten minutes, their time at the door came. She clasped Tyler's arm tight. What if that mean butler from earlier refused to let them in?

She let out a breath when a different gentleman took their invitation at a glance and ushered them inside.

"Guess they aren't too worried about party crashers anymore," Tyler whispered.

"Everyone else looks weirder than we do," she mumbled in response, too captivated by the scenery to put much effort into words.

Palms and ferns coiled around the front entry hall columns, while Japanese lanterns hanging above cast an enchanting glow on the white marble floor and roses erupted from gilded vases and shiny baskets.

"It's like a fairy tale."

At the familiar voice behind them, Fiona whirled.

"Mrs. Easley!"

The older woman winked. "Having a good time, dear?"

"Is something wrong? Is it time to go?" Tyler's arm tightened beneath her fingers.

Mrs. Easley opened a fan made of vibrant blue feathers with a languid swish over her timeless face. "You do worry a good bit, Mr. Robinson. Do you know that?"

The lines around his mouth tightened.

"Oh, now. Don't look so offended. You have a heap of responsibility for one so young, and you carry the weight of everyone around you on your shoulders. But I've already told you your children are fine, and nothing has changed." She fluttered the fan toward him. "Tell me, dear boy, what have you gained by fretting over situations you can't control?"

Rather than waiting for an answer, Mrs. Easley spotted someone at the rear of the entry and waved. Tyler opened his mouth as if to come up with an answer, but Mrs. Easley gave him a knowing look and stepped behind one of the decorated columns. She disappeared a second later.

How did she do that? Fiona craned her neck for any sight of the eccentric innkeeper. Something was special about that lady. Aside from the time-traveling thing, of course. Fiona shook off the strange feeling. She was here to enjoy the ball—the adventure.

Not knowing what else to do, they followed the crowd to a flight of stairs.

"She's wrong, you know," Tyler groused.

"Is she?" Fiona lifted her hem to mount the first stair. "You do spend a lot of time being anxious."

"I have to be." He puffed out a frustrated breath. "No one else at the office keeps up with everything."

"But are you worrying over what has happened or what might happen?"

He grunted as they pivoted to the next flight of steps. "Both."

"Then maybe you'll save yourself from some of the stress if you don't focus on the what-ifs unless they become oh-noes."

His jaw tightened in that way it did when he needed to process something, so she focused on the floating paper lanterns. How incredibly beautiful.

On the third floor, they entered a tropical garden so well done she could forget they were inside. With the walls nowhere to be seen, palms and ferns encased the room, giving the effect of a secret meadow hidden in an impenetrable forest. Palms grazed the ceiling, their fronds draped with orchids. Vines trailed from the ceiling and the door, and lilies and roses climbed the window frames. The entire room smelled of flowers. From somewhere unseen, violin music further sweetened the air.

The room glowed in soft light. Wow. "They have

electricity."

"Huh." Tyler followed her gaze to an antique bulb nestled among the foliage. "Yeah, I guess that's a novelty here."

For a time, they hung near the door and people watched. Three women other than Mrs. Easley had dressed as peacocks, a Roman goddess sashayed past, then some kind of medieval noblewoman, a witch in a pointed hat, and a lady with a stuffed bird in flight on her head. The men came in somewhat less extreme variations of dress—founding fathers in powdered wigs, a sheik, an ironically tall fellow in a Napoleon costume, and another pirate.

Once the room had filled near to capacity, the music ceased, and the partygoers all shifted toward the doorway.

A dark-haired woman paused in the entryway, her dress a sunset of colors. The skirt of white and yellow brocade shifted from deep orange to light canary while a vibrant blue train trimmed in gold trailed her. Long sleeves fell open from her shoulders nearly to the floor, and strings of pearls cascaded from the bodice. An elaborate headdress studded with jewels and gems perched on shiny curls. She welcomed them all to her home, though Fiona barely registered the words.

Alva Vanderbilt. The woman who threw the most expensive party ever seen in her time, all to make sure she became a respected member of society and could rub elbows with the "old money."

This was a magical setting, and Fiona was thrilled to be here. But…wasn't the excess a waste just to impress people whose opinions shouldn't matter?

A thought stirred in her spirit.

Aren't you concerned with what others think of you? Do you not worry they look down on you for choosing to stay home with your children? Do you not push yourself to try to prove your worth to them? Whose opinion counts, child? Mine or theirs?

The breath nearly left her lungs, and she clutched Tyler's arm.

"Are you all right?" The little lines around his eyes tightened.

A weak smile wobbled on her lips, and she had to cement it in place. "I'm good."

At his dubious look, she nodded back to where Alva was still speaking. She said something about a performance and waved her hand in a delicate circle above her head.

People cleared a space in the center of the room.

Fiona moved out of the way, still stuck on the weight of the revelation. Was God trying to show her something? Did she waste her energy worrying over what others thought of her instead of being content with the life God had called her to? Had she become preoccupied with how well she'd decorated her home or how she left the van in a state of disarray? Didn't the root of the issue with her toddler having a meltdown every time they went to the store have more to do with how she thought people were judging her than what was going on with her son? What if she let all that go? If she did her best to love her family well and stop thinking that lack of perfection equaled failure?

Tyler nudged her side and spiked his eyebrows at a woman across the room.

"I've seen pictures of her," Fiona whispered. "She's one of the Vanderbilt family. She's dressed as the Statue of Liberty, I think. Or she called herself something like the Lady of Lights. There's a battery pack and lights in her dress. A huge ordeal in this time. No telling how much it cost."

Tyler opened his mouth to respond, but the arrival of four ghost women snagged his attention. Adorned in snowy fabric with white wigs and powdered faces, they might be trying to be specters or porcelain dolls.

Men in white suits and powdered wigs joined them and arranged themselves in a square with a couple at each corner. When the music started, they bowed and then swapped partners in twirls of satiny fabric. The music intensified, and soon they were a blur of spinning gowns and quick feet. It almost reminded her of a square dance—if square dances had lightning-fast classical music and complicated choreography.

Applause resounded as they finished. The couples bowed to one another and the crowd, not a one out of breath. Fascinating.

The next four dance performances each told an elaborate story with complicated costumes, some of them even moving out of the room and down the staircase. One dance featured women in red-and-black dresses with demon-looking things hanging from the fringe. Totally weird.

After the dances, the orchestra started another tune, and couples swarmed the floor.

Tyler swept back his coattails with a dramatic bow. "Care to dance, my lady?"

Her heart fluttered. "I'd be honored to dance with the most handsome pirate in the room."

"Only the handsomest pirate?" His eyebrow quirked. "You didn't have your eye on that guy in those Robin Hood tights, did you?"

Silly man. She wrinkled her nose as he whisked her toward the middle of the floor. "Well, I have to say those were some interesting pants. I didn't think they made anything tighter than what you're wearing." She winked. "Maybe you should try a pair."

"And lose circulation to my feet? No thanks." He clasped her hand and twirled her around.

The music awakened something within her, and she found herself spinning and swaying with abandon. This is what she'd been missing. Laughing with her best friend, feeling her pulse race at his touch, and savoring butterflies in her stomach. The violinists' bows zipped over the strings, and her feet flew over the polished floor.

It'd been forever since they'd danced. But why? They had music and an open kitchen floor at home. They had a lovely patio under the stars. She could have initiated a dance. Could have met her husband at the door with a kiss and invited him to join her. Instead, she greeted him with a scowl and resentment. A critical spirit.

She caressed the shadow of stubble on his jaw. "I'm sorry I haven't been much fun lately."

Tyler pulled her into a tight spin, and she stumbled. He reached to catch her, but his foot caught on her hem. He steadied her right before she landed in a heap.

"You okay?"

"Yeah." She chuckled. "I just tripped over my own feet and..." Her words faltered as she noticed their surroundings.

Everyone stared. Couples had stopped dancing and cleared a wide space around them. Heat crawled up her neck when a woman in a pink dress designed like an opening rose made a haughty sniff.

"My, what an interesting take on the varsovienne," another woman stated with a heavy dose of snootiness.

The gaggle of women around her made phony attempts at hiding their laughter behind feathered fans.

"Tell me, who was your dance instructor, Mrs....?" the rose woman asked.

A tingle swept up the back of Fiona's neck and

across her face. Her ears throbbed hot.

Tyler tucked her arm in his. "We don't need an instructor to dance together."

The woman tinkled another laugh. A crown of gold and jewels nestled in her mahogany hair. A striking woman, and doubtless someone important.

Fiona tugged on her husband. "Let's go."

He gave the mean woman a flat stare. "I came to dance with my wife."

"By all means." She waved a gloved hand—green with embroidered thorns—toward the dance floor. "Why should you let lack of propriety or pushing others out of your way stop you?"

Fiona tugged on his arm again. "Come on. I'm thirsty anyway."

They strode through the throngs of staring people and the endless maze of potted plants to a table tucked in the back corner next to the band. With each step, her heart rate slowed, and the heat receded from her face. None of those ladies mattered, did they? She smiled at maids in plain dark-blue dresses doling out crystal cups of punch while several in similar attire collected empty glasses from the crowd with such stealth they were almost invisible. Tyler selected two glasses and handed her one.

"That was fun." She tested a sip of the liquid. Chilled sweetness like cold apple cider with hints of cinnamon and orange tripped along her tongue.

"Right up until that woman was so rude."

She was done caring about people like that. "Who cares about her?" She savored another sip. "It's not like we'll ever see her again."

They finished their punch and surrendered the cups to a maid who appeared at their side and then blended back through the greenery.

"Want to take a walk? Scope out the place?" Tyler's soft-as-silk gaze sent a ribbon of pleasure twirling through her center.

"You read my mind." She winked. "I mean, how many people get to say they saw the famous Vanderbilt house during the most elaborate party in history?"

Tyler shrugged. "About a thousand, by the looks of it."

They strolled through the door and down the flight of stairs. The crowd thinned there, though a few people regarded the artwork.

She looped her hand through her husband's elbow. "I want to apologize."

"What for? You didn't mean to stumble. That woman was just mean."

"Not for that." They paused by a painting of a beach scene. "I dropped a lot on you earlier today. I've put all of the blame on you while ignoring my part."

Tyler squeezed her hand, his gaze tender. "I want you to be happy, love." His fingers trailed a gentle path down her cheek. "I'm sorry I've been swamped with this turnover at work."

"I know. But rather than supporting you, I heaped on more guilt. I never should have said you don't care about your family. I know that's not true."

"But it still feels like it." His soft words slumped with the weight of dejection.

"Sometimes, yes," she admitted. "But tonight, I realized I expect you to have energy for me when I don't expect myself to have energy for you. And that's not fair."

He wrapped an arm around her waist. "I'll do better about leaving stuff at work to finish the next day and trying to be home on time. And along with our date nights, I want to give you a night out now and then while I keep the boys. Go do something with the ladies in your Bible study group. I forget I can come home from my job, but yours ends up being more of a twenty-four-seven thing. You need a break too."

"Thank you. And I'll try not to meet you at the door with a frown and a list of annoyances."

"Well, you know, you could always do the Stepford-wife thing at meet me at the door in a dress and heels." He wiggled his eyebrows. "Maybe some stockings…?"

She flashed a coy look. "How about a clean shirt and a smile?"

"Deal." He snugged her against him and kissed her forehead. "Your smile is the most beautiful thing you could wear."

They ambled down the hallway, in no hurry to do anything but enjoy one another's company. They needed this. Date nights and intentional focus on their marriage shouldn't all be on him. She could step up and help with planning. Even if it was only cooking a steak together and dancing in the kitchen after they put the boys to bed.

Just then Mrs. Easley stepped out of a room to their right, waved, lifted her skirt to her knees, and took off at a dead run.

Thirteen

Tyler's feet remained glued to the floor even as he asked, "Should we follow her?"

His wife cast him a you're-crazy look right before snatching up her own skirt and scrambling down the hall. She bounded away like a gazelle, then made a sliding turn around the corner.

Only after the flash of fabric disappeared did his senses return and he rushed after her. His longer legs closed the distance, and he glimpsed Fiona's fiery hair at the bottom of the first landing. He took the stairs two at a time.

Pitching his body around the corner to the next flight down, he'd gained too much momentum to arrest his forward motion even as his brain registered the obstacle in his path.

A tall man in an Abe Lincoln cap. A woman in too many ruffles and flowers clinging to his arm.

Tyler thrust his weight backward, but the effort did little good. He collided with the man. Abe let out a yip, and his hands flew up into the air, dislodging the lady on his arm. Her eyes widened as she tipped backward.

Tyler snagged her arm right before she tumbled head over hoop skirt and yanked her forward. With a cry, she landed on top of him. The air left his lungs in a whoosh. He grunted when the stair treads stabbed into his lower back.

That had been close. Too close.

The woman on his chest wiggled, then let out a horrified screech.

He winced and tried to move her weight off him, but rather than helping, she continued to produce a high-pitched wail that split his eardrums.

Her massive bell-shaped skirt obscured his view of anything beyond the wall of ruffles and fake flowers taking up the majority of the stairwell. Uh-oh. What must the view be like from the lower half of the stairs? Hopefully she'd worn some leggings or whatever equated to them in this time.

Tyler scrambled up, rolling the woman to the side as gently as he could. Once he gained his feet, he offered the red-faced lady assistance.

Abe—or the man dressed as him—slapped Tyler's hand away.

"Do not presume to put hands on my wife! Have you not done enough already Mr.…Mr.—Who *are* you?" The man puffed his chest, his cheeks as red as the woman's who still lay on the stairs exposing everything underneath her skirt.

Tyler made a motion with his chin. "Maybe you should get her up? I doubt she can do it on her own in that getup."

Abe blinked at him, then reached down to help his wife. While they struggled to right her on the stairs, Tyler slipped down the rest of the steps, ignoring the partygoers' shocked expressions.

More people had gathered at the base of the staircase, no doubt drawn by the shrieking, but Fiona and Mrs. Easley were not among them. He wove through the throng of glowering men and whispering women and exited into the front entry with the decorated columns.

He locked gazes with the butler who had tried to kick them out earlier that day. The haughty man's expression darkened as he started Tyler's way.

That would be his cue to skedaddle.

Tyler pivoted in the other direction and ducked behind a palm frond, wove past two maids with trays of rolled napkins, and slipped through an unlocked door.

He let out a breath. That was close. Didn't need that stuffed shirt tossing him on his ear before he could find Fiona.

No sooner had the wind left his lungs in relief than he sucked it back in.

Uh-oh.

An entire room full of suited men with matching cigars in one hand and brandy glasses in the other all surveyed him.

He straightened and tugged on the lapels of his pirate jacket. Something poked at his rib. He'd forgotten all about the masks he'd put in his pocket. Might need to use his after this debacle.

"Good evening, gentlemen. Sorry to have disturbed you." He grabbed the knob.

"One moment." The voice halted Tyler's momentum. "I don't believe we've met."

Dressed in a double-breasted black jacket and red cravat studded with a diamond, the speaker didn't look like he'd participated in the costume part of this ball. Unless that was his costume. He'd parted his hair down the middle and tamed what wanted to be dark curls underneath shiny hair gel.

"Didn't mean to interrupt," Tyler said. "I was looking for my wife, who clearly isn't in here. So I'll be on my way."

An older man with a thick gray mustache elbowed the first. "Look here, Willie. I'd say that wife of yours invited folk from every corner of the city to make sure *the* Mrs. Astor felt the pinch of being left out."

His companions chortled at his emphasis of the word *the*.

Tyler shifted his feet, trying to piece together the information he'd gained from Fiona. He cleared his throat. "Mr. Vanderbilt. Nice house. Thanks for inviting me."

Before the man could respond, Tyler opened the

door and hurried out, closing it behind him.

Voices came from the room across the hall, and the familiar timbre of a fiery redhead caught his ear through the cracked door. He grasped a golden knob and eased it forward to get a better look.

Fiona stood in the center of another opulent room, hands on her hips. He widened the door to take in Mrs. Easley standing across from her, features set in a gleeful expression his wife didn't share.

"There you are. What's happening?" Tyler moved into the room and closed the door.

Both women eyed him. Neither responded.

"What's wrong?"

Mrs. Easley clicked her tongue. "Don't be so quick to assume trouble, dear boy." Distracted, her focus bounced around the room.

He shot her a sour look, though she didn't notice. What was she looking for? "Most people would assume a person running away to have encountered some kind of trouble."

Fiona snorted. "I told her the same thing. She found it funny."

Tyler regarded the older woman as she tilted her head, appearing lost in her thoughts. "So nothing's wrong. You just decided to...what? Practice for a marathon in the middle of a ball?"

She glanced toward the ceiling with a rueful smile. "Snarky one, isn't he?"

Tyler and Fiona shared a look. Who was she talking to?

Mrs. Easley faced them and clasped her hands. "I thank you for being concerned for me. It is rather sweet of you. But no, all is well. We merely needed to hurry in order to balance a couple of assignments all at once. Timing is everything, you know."

Before either of them could respond, a bell chimed from out in the hallway.

"Ah, yes. Speaking of timing." Mrs. Easley swept into a graceful curtsy. "That's my cue to go. You'll find what you need over there." She gestured toward the fireplace at the rear.

Fireplace might be an understatement. Fire*wall*, more like. It had to be at least nine feet across and a good five tall. Who would want something like that in his house? Where children could walk inside.

"What are we…?" He swallowed. The woman had disappeared.

Fiona's eyes widened. "Weird, right? She keeps doing that."

"No weirder than anything else happening to us today." Had they really left their normal life just this morning? It already seemed like a week ago.

Fiona scooped something from the floor. A folded scrap of paper. She opened it and scanned the contents.

"What is it?"

She handed it over. "A clue maybe? Oh, are we

going on a scavenger hunt?"

He focused on the page.

> Once upon the midnight hour,
>
> When the fire lay cold and bare,
>
> Was the key to finding the way back home,
>
> Lest the adventurers might despair.
>
> Divulge the list and take the tome,
>
> Donning the cloak of mystery,
>
> Or in the past, all will remain,
>
> Lost to history.

His fingers crunched the edges of the page. "She can't be serious."

"What?" Fiona reread the words shaking in his hand.

"What do you mean, 'what'? It's right here!" He shook the page. "It says if we don't do whatever it is she wants, then we are going to be stuck in the past."

"It doesn't say that." Frowning, she plucked the page from his fingers. "It says we are supposed to find a tome so it doesn't get lost to history."

"No. It says the adventurers will despair, stuck in the past, and lost to history."

She shook her head. "It can't mean that. I mean, she promised we'd go home. Right?"

He wanted to agree, but the sinking feeling in his gut said this dream thing had just become a nightmare.

Fourteen

This couldn't be happening. Fiona read the lines again, looking for different meanings, but now that Tyler had put the idea in her head, she couldn't dislodge it.

"We need to find her and ask." She took two steps before he grabbed her wrist to stop her.

"That's only wasting time. You know how that woman disappears. We won't see her unless she wants us to."

Fiona tugged her lower lip through her teeth. "Okay. Well, the first thing is the fireplace, right? That seems pretty obvious. 'Once upon the midnight hour, when the fire lay cold and bare, was the key to finding the way back home.'"

From the hallway, the clock chimed again.

"How many was that?" Tyler asked. "I'm guessing it's chiming midnight."

"Once upon the midnight hour. I wonder what that means. Is it like once upon a time, or does it mean something only happens once—at midnight?"

Tyler's forehead crinkled. "She did say something about us being here on time. We better hurry."

They scrambled over to the fireplace and started searching. The stacked bricks formed a cave big enough to be a child's playhouse. If children didn't mind being covered in soot. Which they didn't, of course. Children had no worries about ruined clothes or heaps of laundry. They lived in the moment.

Fiona hiked her skirt up and kicked off her satiny flats.

"What are you doing?"

"I doubt we are going to find anything standing out here."

Ignoring his incredulous stare, she shed the outer dress with the puffy sleeves and tossed it over the back of a gold-upholstered couch. Then she pulled the hem of the white dress to her waist and knotted it, leaving the length to fall midthigh. Watching for sharp objects underfoot, she ducked inside the fireplace.

Tyler moved to the edges where he inspected the joints of the surrounding mantel.

If she were a mysterious woman leaving clues, where would she hide something? She wrinkled her nose. That was a stupid question. She wouldn't be hiding anything inside a fireplace, for one thing. Not to mention a fireplace belonging to an opulent mansion in the middle of a multimillion-dollar costume ball.

In 1883.

She let out a huff of air, and the ashes stirred. This was ridiculous. Utterly insane. There was nothing in here but cold embers, ash, and remnants of firewood. She turned to exit when a shiny flicker caught her eye.

Above the center of the opening, just below where the headspace curved to allow for the flue, a square of copper metal huddled where a brick should be.

"Hey, hon? I found something."

Tyler stuck in his head and twisted for a better look, trying to see while staying out of the ashes. Giving up, he shifted to join her inside, ducking to gain the necessary clearance. "How'd you even see that in the dark?"

"There was a glint."

He rolled his eyes with an of-course-there-would-be expression. As deep as they were in this craziness, a random glint of light when there *was* no light wasn't the strangest thing to happen. Might as well go with it.

He stuck a finger under the edge of the metal, and it swung free on hinges, revealing a niche. He extracted a rectangular object wrapped in oiled cloth.

"Looks like a notebook." He ducked out and offered a sooty hand to help her. "The poem said something about a tome. Maybe this counts."

She cleared the soot and traversed the cold marble, leaving dark footprints. "I always thought of a tome as a giant book. You know, some big hefty thing like they only have in the national library."

"Or like Mrs. Easley had on her desk."

"Right. Like that." Fiona caught herself before she smeared her hands down her hips and ruined the white dress. Her hands were filthy.

She almost told Tyler to wipe his hands before he opened the book, but he already had the string untied and was unwinding the oilcloth. The brown covering fell back, revealing a dark leather-bound book wrapped and tied with a leather cord. He undid the string, opened the book, and flipped through. "It's empty."

"Let me see." She slid it from his hands and thumbed through the pages. Every one of them blank. "I don't get it. How is this the key home? Maybe we found the wrong thing."

He fished out Mrs. Easley's note and read the poem again. "'Once upon the midnight hour, when the fire lay cold and bare.' Okay, so we got that. It's midnight, and we went into where the fire is cold."

Fiona pointed to the next part. "'Lest the adventurers might despair.' What do you think that means?"

"I don't know. Despair about getting back home? The next line talks about finding the list and taking the tome. Maybe we missed the list."

He handed her the note and reentered the fireplace. After scrounging around, he reemerged even dirtier. "There's nothing else in there. No list."

Fiona flipped through the pages again. "No list in

here, either."

"Wait. It said divulge the list. Does that mean find it or share it? But share it with who?" Tyler scratched the back of his head and groaned. "What about that other part? The cloak of mystery?"

"Not *cloak* like what a knight wears. It's more metaphorical. Like camouflage, maybe?"

He snapped his fingers. "I had forgotten about these until I ran into Mr. Vanderbilt."

"Wait. You met Mr. Vanderbilt? When?"

"When I was chasing you through the house." He plucked the masks from his pocket. "Maybe she means these?"

Having forgotten all about the Venetian-style masks, she accepted the feathered one. A little worse for wear, but not too bad for having spent the day inside his pocket. "Maybe. These would be a cloak of mystery, I guess. But no one knows who we are anyway, so there's no point."

"About that." He ran a hand through his hair, smudging ash on his forehead. "I had a, um, *situation* on the stairs."

"What sort of situation?"

"The kind where I made a woman in a Mary Lincoln dress end up with her hoops in the air."

Her jaw dropped. "You what?"

"I didn't mean to. I ran into them while chasing you, and when she started to fall backward, I caught her, and she came forward instead. Did you know that skirt is like a giant bell?" He puckered his lips. "I sure hope she wore some pants or something under there."

She could only gawk. Then a seed of mirth at the absurdity of how that must have looked sprouted in her chest. She put her hand to her mouth, but the laughter burst free. Soon she was clutching her side and gasping for breath. "You...and she...? Oh my word. What about the people on the stairs?"

Tyler chortled. "They did all look pretty shocked when I passed them. Then I ran into that lemon-mouthed butler, you know, the one who wouldn't let us in the first time."

Her laughter faded. "Oh no. That probably didn't go well."

"He didn't look too happy to see me, so I ducked into the room across the hall." He gestured with his chin. "That's when I met Mr. Vanderbilt, who made it clear he didn't know me."

Not good. They couldn't get kicked out while they had this riddle to solve. "If we wash off all this soot, you take off the jacket and that sword, and I shed this top part of the dress and just keep the white one under-neath, maybe—with the masks—we'll look like different people. There's so many guests here they might not notice."

"The kitchen was in the back near where we came in with the flowers, wasn't it?"

"What about the clues, though?" She eyed the fire-place, willing it to cough up more secrets. "We still haven't found the list. Or the key."

"What key?"

"It says 'the key to finding the way back home.'"

"Maybe the fireplace was the key to finding the way back home."

Fiona studied the structure. "I doubt the fireplace is a time portal."

"This is why I hate English." Tyler pinched the bridge of his nose, leaving more black smudges.

"What does English have to do with it?"

"This is like English class in school. Trying to figure out the meaning of Shakespeare and all that. If people would write what they mean instead of trying to be poetic about it, then we might know what they were talking about."

She opened her mouth to refute him, but in this particular instance, she agreed. "We can figure this out. 'The key to finding the way home, lest the adventurers might despair. Divulge the list and take the tome. Don—or wear—the cloak of mystery,' which we think are the masks. Then the last part says, 'or in the past, all will remain, lost to history.' Hopefully, that means the list and the tome, maybe even the masks, will remain lost to history. Not the adventurers."

Tyler drew a long breath, thoughts churning behind his eyes.

She waited for a few heartbeats, but when he didn't offer any insights, she prompted, "What do you think? Should we get cleaned up or keep looking?"

After another thoughtful pause, he rubbed at a smudge on his palm, smearing it further. "We should wash up and do the costume change before someone finds us."

"But what about the list? We might want to finish looking before we leave this room, right?"

He regarded her. "Why do you do that?"

"Do what?" Her mind started wandering to where they should look next. Maybe the blank book was the key that would send them to the tome and list. But how, since it was blank?

"You ask me a question, and I give you an answer. And then you ask me again, usually in a different way, until you get me to give you the answer you wanted. Why ask me at all?"

She stopped and focused on him. "I don't do that."

"You just did. You asked if I thought we should get cleaned up or keep looking. I gave you my answer, but it must not have been the one you already had in mind."

"I…" She closed her lips. She did do that. Last weekend she asked him if he wanted to run errands before or after lunch and he'd said after, but then she'd asked him three more times, in different ways, because the correct answer had been before. Before the boys needed naps.

"If you already know what you want, then say so. You don't need to ask me, hoping I'll agree with you so it looks like I made the decision and not you."

Whoa. Her mouth slid open as she blinked. She didn't do that. Except…she did. "I'm sorry."

He reached for her, then noticed the soot and let his hand drop. "You know I'll give you what you want, love. But if what you want is for me to make the decision, then please respect the answer I give you when I do."

"I'll do better." She parroted the words he'd used earlier.

If nothing else, this trip had forced a lot of conversations they avoided. Maybe that was the key to ironing out the wrinkles in their marriage. Talking about the issues instead of brushing them aside in hopes they'd go away.

"This night has been good for us," she began. "From now on we should—"

The door burst open, and a stink-eyed butler stomped inside.

Fifteen

"You two!" The steaming butler pointed at them. "You're not—"

Tyler stepped in front of Fiona to shield her. "I beg your pardon!"

On the verge of spewing accusations, the bug-eyed man halted with his mouth still open.

"This is how Willie lets his employees behave?" Tyler gave a rueful shake of his head. "For shame, I say."

Fiona stifled a giggle. He struggled to keep an indignant expression. If he had any hope of maintaining this farce, he couldn't laugh. Even if the man flushed a deep shade of red and his eyes bulged.

The butler tugged his jacket lapels, accusing gaze sweeping over Tyler and probing Fiona.

Best to redirect the man while Tyler still had control of this situation. He squared his shoulders and mustered a commanding voice. "As you can see, I require a moment of privacy. Kindly step away. Then you and I shall go have a talk with Willie."

The butler's eyebrows looked like they were trying to compete in aerobics—scrunching and releasing in a rhythmic fashion as his brain worked out what Tyler had said. No doubt he had wanted to either make Tyler leave or take him to his boss. He hadn't been expecting Tyler to suggest the same. And get him in trouble.

"Well?" Tyler waved toward the door. "Be gone with you, man!"

The butler snapped his mouth shut, whirled on his heel, and strode from the room, closing the door behind him.

"Speaking of Shakespeare!" Fiona burst into laughter. "That was great! Where did you learn to act like that?"

He shrugged. "Most of the time, if you appear confident, people will respond. I've had to use that with a variety of contractors and engineers on the job."

She nudged him with her shoulder. "I'm impressed. Glad I could see you in action."

Heat surged through his chest, and he couldn't help straightening his posture. Nothing boosted a man's confidence like impressing the woman he loved.

"We better hurry," he said. "I doubt he'll wait for long before deciding to come after the sooty pirate."

Fiona's gaze snagged on the heavy drapery. "They have a good cleaning service, right?"

"Why?" He followed her line of sight. "You aren't

going to make a dress out of the curtains, are you? Like in *Gone with the Wind*? We don't have time for that." He was only half-joking.

She rolled her eyes. "I was thinking more like using them as a towel to wipe away the soot."

At his nod, they hurried to the nearest window and used the velvet curtains to scrub their hands. Fiona took a corner and rubbed at his face.

"We need some water." She spotted a vase and brightened.

He caught her. "No time. Let's put on the masks."

They secured masks over their soiled faces. Then she untied her hem from around her waist. She grabbed her shoes from by the fireplace and tugged them on, hopping on one foot in her haste. Tyler shed the pirate jacket and slid the sword and its scabbard off his belt. He refastened the belt and stashed the sword, his jacket, and the top layer of Fiona's dress behind a dainty couch.

"Now what?" Fiona whispered. "There's only one door out of here."

"Maybe." He scanned the walls. "These mansions are all about having ways for servants to slip around unnoticed, right?" The maids had appeared and disappeared among the guests with uncanny stealth.

"Smart. There's gotta be a servant entrance some-where."

They split up, each taking one side of the room. Soon he found what they needed.

"Over here," he whispered as loudly as he dared.

She darted to him, the feathers on her white-and-gold mask bouncing with each step.

A hidden door made to look like a section of the wall with the doorknob camouflaged within the wainscoting was their mode of escape.

His wife flashed a charming grin and tugged the door open, creating a puff of air. With one glance back at the room, he followed her into a tight hallway. Gone were the fancy decorations and expensive furniture. Drab gray walls and heavy gloom existed in the hidden corridors.

He pulled the door closed, leaving only an outline of light to mark the room they'd left. The butler would be familiar with this space and guess what they'd done. Tyler unfastened his belt. Maybe he could buy extra time.

"What are you doing?" An incredulous note raised her whisper.

"It won't take them but a second to figure out where we've gone. Why not buy ourselves a little time?" But how he'd accomplish that with only a belt for rope remained to be seen.

She sidled closer. "Too bad we don't have a flashlight. That would make whatever you're planning easier."

That gave him an idea. They had to have some kind of lighting in here. He felt along the side of the wall.

Bingo. Wall sconce with a gaslight. No one had bothered to light it tonight, but it might still serve his purpose.

He looped the belt around the doorknob and then stretched the other end to the wall fixture.

And came up short.

Fiona laid her hand on his arm. "Great idea, but we should hurry out of here. We can be in a different part of the house before they come this way."

Good point. He tugged the belt free and took her hand. He replaced his belt while they crept down the hallway until they came to a *T* juncture. When he tried to picture the layout of the house, he ended up guessing and veered left.

Fiona followed, her soft shoes scraping along the stone floor. At the end of the hall, he paused and listened. Feeble light seeped around the door seams. If he hadn't nearly run into it in the dark, he'd have missed the exit.

After feeling around at the approximate level, he found the knob and eased the door open.

Heat sprung through the opening, but the room beyond remained silent. He stepped out and tugged Fiona with him.

"Where are we?" She peeked around his shoulder.

Muted laughter and music drifted from somewhere else in the house, indicating they were a good distance from the party.

He scanned the tubs and lines of drying linens. No one would be doing anything in here during the ball. "I'm guessing the laundry room."

Were they going to have to sneak around the rest of the night? He flexed his fingers. So much for giving Fiona her Cinderella ball.

"That was awesome." She bounced on her toes.

"Really?" He regarded her in the dim light. "You liked digging around in a fireplace and running from a butler more than dancing in a fancy dress?"

She smirked. "We did the dancing part, and that was great. But now we get to do the adventure part, and that's even better. Think about the story we'll have once we get home. Not that anyone would believe us, obviously. But we'll know."

Her enthusiasm seeped into him. He gathered her in his arms. "You're amazing, you know that?"

"Well…" She drew the word out in a teasing fashion.

Whatever else she might have been about to say, he couldn't wait for. He needed to kiss his wife. His spunky, adventurous, amazing wife. Cupping her jaw, he drew her lips to his. Her arms slipped around his neck, and she returned his passion in equal measure. He lost himself in the beauty of her until he had to put his hands on her waist and separate his lips from hers.

She looked up at him through her lashes. "That part's a pretty good adventure."

"The best adventure, in my book." He clasped her hand and grinned. "But one we should continue later."

Fiona snagged two dish towels from a hook and dipped the ends in the nearest tub of water. They made quick work of scrubbing their hands and faces as best they could in the meager light.

It would have to do.

As clean as possible given the circumstance, they slipped through the lines of rolled napkins and past temporary walls of hanging tablecloths to a door into an empty hallway. This one clearly meant for the more affluent with the gilded mirrors and marble floors. Electric sconces spaced evenly down the wall offered better lighting, so they adjusted their clothes and masks.

Fiona ran a hand down her skirt. "Do I look okay?"

"Stunning, love." He placed a quick kiss on her cheek since he couldn't trust himself to the temptation of her rosy lips again. The last thing they needed was that stuffy butler to find them making out in the hallway.

"You still have the book, right?" She redirected his thoughts.

He plucked the item from where he'd stashed it in his rear waistband. "Come up with any more ideas?"

"Just one." She opened the back cover. A satisfied tilt curved her lips. "I got to thinking while we were scrambling down the hall. We only flipped through the pages. We didn't look at the covers."

He took the book and inspected the blocky words on the back of the last page.

> If you are reading this, then I am not the last.
>
> Hopefully, this means I made it home after all.
>
> Pray that I did, fellow traveler. I believe God exists outside of time, so all prayers count.

Tyler shared a look with Fiona. "Do you think another time traveler left this?"

"Seems that way." She pursed her lips. "But this house was just built, if I remember right from history. This ball is Alva's housewarming party."

"What about a time loop? Say this person came here from, like, the 1940s or something. They could have been here and gone back yesterday."

"Or they could be here now."

The words hung between them. What if people from several eras were all here at once? Who would know, given all the costumes?

She released a slow breath. "That kinda makes my brain hurt."

He agreed. They refocused on the page.

> There's too much to risk getting lost in the details, so I'll keep it simple in

hopes I might help you.

Every traveler goes on this journey for a purpose. Yours is unique to you.

The key to going home is knowing why you came in the first place.

Your own list, you might say.

When I found this book, it was filled with entries. The only available space for me to write was here on the back of this final page. But as soon as I started writing, the others disappeared.

I don't know how to explain it. Only that it is true. Perhaps because I thought to draw from their inspiration and need only my own. I know not if you will see the other entries or even if you will see this one. But if you do, here is what I discovered:

Each page held the reason they came. Such as to find out if they were ready for commitment or to break past barriers keeping them from following their calling and the like.

Pick a page and write your truth. Then find a place to tuck the book away, ready for the next traveler. You'll know where. I'll pray for you.

God bless.

Fiona stepped away and tapped her chin. "Wow."

Yeah. He didn't know what to make of it. "That must be the list from the poem."

"Right. We make our own and add it inside. Then we hide the book somewhere?"

"And if we don't, we don't go home?"

So much for Mrs. Easley's promise. They were on their own.

They locked eyes, neither having an answer.

"Maybe there's a clue or—" She gasped. "It's gone!"

"What?" He looked back at the page he'd just read. "It's blank."

He thumbed through again, and this time, words appeared each time he flipped the page. They disappeared again as soon as he moved on.

"Stop. Let me see." Fiona took the book. "Let's just pick one."

She opened to a random page, and he peered over her shoulder to read along.

> This is Sarah. I'm supposed to write out a list. Reasons why I came here. I hope that means I can go home soon because Pa has got to be worried by now. This party sure is something fine, and I thought it would be everything I always wanted. But it's not. I've learned what I really want.
>
> The meadow behind our farm

where Billy takes me to listen to the creek when I'm upset. The sound of Ma's beautiful voice in church every Sunday morning and the sweet harmony of my baby sisters. Dancing with Billy after a barn raising even though I'm only wearing homespun. And knowing he don't care whether I'll never have a silk gown like the one I have on now.

I want the life God meant for me instead of the one I was going to throw everything away for. What I really wanted was at home all along.

She flipped to the next page, but once again, they were all blank.

Crazy. "I wonder how many times these pages have been written over. How many stories are in here?"

She ran a finger down the empty page and shook her head. "What are we going to write?"

A weight settled in his stomach. Would he doom them if he got the wrong answer? "We've had a chance to talk about a lot of things since we've been here."

"I'd thought the same. That's something for the list."

Right. A good start. "I've learned I let my job take too high of a priority and often I don't hear what you are saying because, instead of listening to understand,

I'm listening to defend. All this time, I've missed what you meant. Your love language is quality time spent together, and without it, you are left feeling like you don't matter."

The glimmer in her eyes spilled down her cheeks. He brushed her tear away with his thumb.

She drew a shaky breath and pressed his hand against her cheek, leaning into his palm. "And I've learned I put the entire burden of my joy and happiness on you, which isn't fair. I've let myself become resentful of the life I prayed to have." Her voice hitched, and she cleared her throat. The fingers resting over his hand trembled. "Instead of thinking you can read my mind and know what I want and need, I should tell you."

He caressed her cheek. "Life is supposed to have adventure mixed in. If we spend so much energy on making a living that we forget to *live,* then we are missing out on all the blessings God has for us."

She nodded, and for the first time in a long while, he felt like they were on the same page. That they had connected on a deep level.

"I love you, Tyler Robinson."

The breathy words washed over him and stirred a deep sense of protectiveness for his wife's heart. A heart that was his privilege to lead and to cherish. He could only pray God would give him the grace to do both well.

"I love you too, my feisty Fiona."

Her sigh broke the spell hanging between them, and her hand slid from atop his. "Guess all we need now is a pen."

She looked down at the page and started to laugh. "At this point, I don't even know why I'm surprised." She tipped the book toward him, displaying the new words printed on the page.

You found your list and took the tome,

Starting the journey home.

Now hide this book,

Up in a nook.

When dessert is served at two.

He closed the book and tucked it in his waistband. "Looks like we are off to dinner."

Sixteen

*E*xcitement tingled through Fiona as she and Tyler followed the line of people heading for the main floor dining room. The soaring ceilings in the grand hall opposite the staircase dripped with crystal chandeliers, and their light glinted off the French gilding lining mirrors, molding, and furniture. No wonder they called it the "Gilded Age" when the rich not only coated their homes but their very lives in layers of gold.

She even matched in her white gown and the white-and-gold mask that now made her look less Regency and more fanciful Venetian maiden. Tyler looked pretty good in those fitted pants and billowy shirt.

The lavishness was interesting. But a part of her wondered about the opulent display. What else could Alva have done with that much money?

Fiona squeezed Tyler's arm. "You know what we have is enough, right?"

His steps slowed. "What do you mean?"

"We have a comfortable home and a nice life. I take

a few coupons to the grocery store, but I never have to worry if we can feed our children. I don't know if I thank you enough for all you have done to make that possible. But I also want you to know I am content. I don't long for"—she gestured with her chin at a gaudy golden vase—"all of this."

He chuckled. "That's good. If you were looking for Vanderbilt money, then you married the wrong guy."

She playfully bumped his shoulder. "You know what I mean. I don't want you thinking I expect you to work yourself to death so we can have a fancier car or house."

He regarded her before smiling and squeezing her hand on his arm. "Thanks, love."

She'd suspected he thought something similar, but the relief in his eyes pinched her heart. She needed to work on not complaining when everything wasn't perfect and focusing on all she was grateful for.

Sorry, Lord. Help me to do better.

They passed underneath a marble arch and into a daunting space arrayed with elegant tables. The stained glass window towering over the room would have been stunning in the daylight. Gothic-style wainscoting rose taller than her head, topped with stone walls. At the double fireplace, life-sized female marble sculptures supported an oak mantle on their heads. A gallery across the room featured an orchestra playing soft music.

She'd thought Tyler had been exaggerating when

he'd guessed more than a thousand people were here, but with so many tables awaiting the guests, he might be right. White linen cloths covered each one topped with crystal goblets and enough plates and utensils to make her nervous. Centered on each dinner plate, a gold-rimmed placement card marked a guest's name.

Her stomach clenched. "Do you think we have those?"

"We should. We have an invitation."

She eyed the cards as they moved around the edge of the room. "That might have been a fake, you know."

"If we don't have a seat, then we'll slip out. All we have to do is wait for dessert, right?"

"And find a nook. What does that even mean? I don't see how a hiding place has anything to do with dessert."

The other guests all seemed to have an innate sense of where to go since they filed into the room and peeled off into general sections before locating their place and taking their seats.

"Ah. I think I get it." She dipped her chin.

"Get what?" he asked as they made their way forward.

She tugged him to a stop. "We'll be in the back. See the Vanderbilt family up there?"

He followed her gaze. A single table stretched along the far wall underneath the stained glass window. "Yep. That's the dude I saw when I was looking for you."

"So this is going to be medieval style. The most important people go to the front. Notice how everyone has a general idea about what part of the room they are in? They all know where they fall on the social ladder. We will be on the bottom if we are here at all. No reason to draw attention by getting too close to tonight's royalty."

They turned back the way they came, cut past the archway, and inspected the rearmost table in the room's left corner. Her shoulders loosened as she approached two place cards marked as Mr. and Mrs. Robinson at the last seats available before the wall.

Tyler pulled her chair for her before sitting in the adjacent one.

"This is great," she said. "We can see everyone from here, and fewer people will notice us."

He raised an eyebrow in that cute way he had. "Good call. Though you're probably the only woman here who would think so, given what you told me about the seating chart."

At least they had a spot at one of the tables. Her stomach rumbled. Those steaks had been great, but that had been over five hours ago.

With four other places, their table accommodated six, and soon a new couple in their mid-forties joined them. The man had dressed in what Fiona could only guess was a Louis XIV costume, what with the blue coat embroidered with gold fleur-de-lis and the fur-lined cloak.

The woman on his arm must be Marie Antoinette, though who would choose to wear a powdered wig topped with a wooden sailboat? Must be a pain to keep balanced, but she had great posture.

The gentleman held out her chair, and they settled in the seats to Tyler's left. "Good evening." The man spoke while the woman offered a nod. "I don't believe we've met. I'm Mr. Fredrick Morris, and this is my wife, Mrs. Angeline Morris."

"Good evening," Tyler repeated. "I'm Tyler Robinson, and this is my wife, Fiona."

Angeline tilted her head, but she must have felt the weight of her ship shift. She straightened. "Those are rather unusual names, don't you think so, Mr. Morris? Surely we would have remembered. Is this your first visit to the city?"

"We've never been to New York before." Tyler plucked his napkin from the ring and spread it on his lap.

Mr. Morris tapped a finger on the table. "How splendid your first foray would be to the grandest ball of the year."

"Yes." Fiona fixed a smile in place though she didn't care for his snide tone. "Splendid indeed."

The next couple arrived, saving her from further probing questions that would expose them as high-society frauds.

Beside her, Tyler went rigid as the other two remained standing behind their chairs and basted him in frosty stares.

Uh-oh.

That had to be old Abe and his wife, Mary Todd Lincoln. The people Tyler had upended on the stairs. Their attempt at a costume change and the addition of the mask didn't seem to have disguised Tyler enough. The man raised his nose in the air, and the woman fanned a hand at her throat.

They did bear an interesting resemblance to the actual historical couple. The man wouldn't match Lincoln's six foot four, but he had a lean face to his wife's round one and a rail-thin body type to her curvier figure. She even had the same dark hair as Mrs. Lincoln.

Mr. Morris rose, and Fiona elbowed Tyler to do the same. That was a thing. Men stood when a woman joined them. He should have done that when the first couple arrived. At least they hadn't been rude about it. Too much, anyway. No wonder all these people kept suspecting they didn't belong. They had to have committed over a dozen social missteps that identified them as frauds.

Abe settled his wife, and then all three men took a seat. Mary plucked a fan from somewhere in her voluminous skirts and fanned her red cheeks.

"About what happened on the stairs," Tyler said. "I'm sorry. It was…most unfortunate."

Abe grunted. "I should say so." He focused on the man across from him. "Mr. Morris, have you ever made the acquaintance of these two?"

"Mr. and Mrs. Robinson," Mr. Morris supplied. "I've not had the pleasure until this evening."

"I'm Tyler and this is Fiona."

The man held his gaze for a few heartbeats before propriety won over. "John and Patricia Pembroke."

An awkward silence settled until an army of servants arrived with the first course. A man with a silver tray approached and set crystal bowls onto their place settings while another poured champagne into each flute.

Fiona waited until they had both left and Mrs. Lincoln—no, Pembroke—removed the lid from the petite dish. Her eyes lit up.

Following suit, she and Tyler lifted the lids on theirs as well.

Her stomach lurched.

Caviar!

She replaced the lid and set the dish to the side.

"Madam doesn't care for the caviar?" a waiter asked, appearing from thin air behind her.

Fiona startled at his nearness, and her hand went to her pounding heart. "Oh! You—"

Her champagne flute toppled into the plate to the right of her water goblet and spilled across the table. Mortification raced up her neck as she struggled to remove her linen napkin from her lap and catch the liquid before it reached Mary Lincoln's dress.

The waiter, who could have been a stunt double for the Flash, contained the trickle before it could cause irreparable damage.

Mrs. Pembroke glared at her.

Fiona squeaked out an apology and did her best to maintain an air of calm as she addressed the kind man who had saved her from further humiliation. "Thank you for catching that. I'm sorry to be so clumsy."

"Of course, madam." The man, whose smooth face pegged him somewhere in his twenties, blinked at her. He tucked the wet rag behind his back and left with a bow.

Tyler leaned close. "It's okay. There're too many dishes on this table anyway. Could have happened to anyone."

She doubted that, but appreciated the sentiment all the same.

The other diners dipped their spoons into the caviar and removed a few black beads.

"Looks like we should have taken smaller bites," Tyler whispered. "Want to try it again?"

Not in a million years. Her stomach revolted just thinking about it. She gave him the slightest headshake.

The other couples soon forgot their presence and fell into conversation among themselves. Content to listen and observe this slice of history, Fiona kept her hands in her lap and her eyes focused on her plate until the next course.

Mr. Morris spoke of railroads and Western expansion in general terms, and the two women seemed fascinated by the weather. Either high society was dull or they'd been placed at the dud table. Fiona withheld a smirk when the topic shifted from the weather to the latest hat fashion—*and* how it would hold up in the coming weather.

The waiters next arrived with a cold pea soup she sampled and then set aside, followed by a tray that contained three round shells.

She cast a look at her husband. He blinked at his plate and then caught her eye.

"Snails?" he mouthed.

Had to be. Especially since they came with shrimp forks. Fish eggs and now snails. What she wouldn't give for a slice of pepperoni pizza and a root beer. Her stomach rumbled, and she pushed her palm against it in an attempt to cover the noise.

Mr. Pembroke plucked a hunk of meat from one of the shells and popped it into his mouth. His wife glanced at Fiona and caught her watching.

"Unsure how to proceed?" Her saccharine smile warred with disapproving eyes. "One does have to ask what sort of balls you are used to at home. Which would be...?"

Fiona straightened her posture and gave the other

woman a flat look through her feathered mask. "I do not care for the taste of fish eggs or snails."

The woman sniffed and resumed her conversation with Mrs. Morris. This time they droned on about shoes.

Finally, something Fiona could eat arrived. A plate of cheeses and cubes of bread. She did her best to eat slowly, but they soon disappeared.

"At this rate, this is going to be a sixteen-course meal," Tyler quipped.

Their tablemates did not find the joke amusing.

"This is to be the finest ball of the season," Mr. Morris supplied. "So I am not surprised Mrs. Vanderbilt would wish to treat her guests well at such a joyous occasion as celebrating her new home."

Fiona couldn't help an unladylike snort. "That woman used this party to force Mrs. Astor into accepting the Vanderbilts into the 400. With all the newspapers covering the story and it becoming the talk of the city, Caroline couldn't let her dear daughter be the only girl not invited to this soirée."

Everyone gaped at her. Everyone except Tyler, of course, who couldn't contain his laugh.

"Really." Mrs. Pembroke's eyelids fluttered as she gasped the word.

Mrs. Morris's lips flattened into an unappealing line.

Oh good gracious. These people were ridiculous. Fiona pointedly faced her husband. "Tomorrow, we're getting pizza."

"You read my mind, love."

More than an hour later, after more courses of shrimp, weird pudding-like concoctions, a variety of vegetables, duck, lamb, and what she suspected to be liver, they got to the finger bowls of water meant for cleaning. Which must mean dessert would soon be on the way.

The waiters all arrived at once, a swarm of them in matching uniforms. They placed the dishes down with a flourish. Each plate contained a puffy ball of meringue she'd only ever seen on cooking shows.

Oh no. That wasn't going to be Baked Alaska, was it?

She hoped not. Because setting her dessert on fire would surely be a recipe for a massive disaster.

Seventeen

$\mathcal{A}$ waiter lit a fire in a pot and then poured the flaming liquid onto the frothy dessert in front of Tyler. Dozens of men and women dressed in similar attire did the same all around the room. During the fascinating process, Fiona sat stiff as a board, hands clasped in her lap. After she'd spilled the champagne and the mishaps at Delmonico's earlier today...well, he couldn't blame her. She'd die of embarrassment if she set the table on fire.

Once the flames sputtered out, the delighted guests poked their spoons into toasted meringue.

Tyler picked up his fork and nudged her to do the same. "Might as well try it."

Her narrowed-eyed look said he should remember what had happened last time she'd sampled something new.

He bent in with a reassuring nudge. "How bad can sugar be?"

With a shrug, she picked up a spoon and cut into

the outer crust. He did the same. Inside, sponge cake surrounded a scoop of ice cream. He took a taste. Pretty good.

Fiona seemed to enjoy hers as well, and soon the last bite disappeared. The woman across from her raised her eyebrows, leaving half of her own to go to waste.

Few things soured him like pretentious people. He ignored their tablemates and twisted in his chair to face his wife. "It's around two o'clock, and we've had dessert. But I don't see...you know."

Her gaze roamed the room. "Me either. It said a nook, but that could be almost anywhere."

The room grew quiet as Alva Vanderbilt rose and thanked everyone for joining them for dinner, then invited the guests to return to dancing.

They waited as Mrs. Lincoln struggled to remove her hoop skirts from underneath the table. Tyler didn't bother to stand while the women rose and the other two men followed suit. Neither couple offered goodbyes.

Tyler and Fiona remained seated as the guests filed out, lingering until only the waiters and a swarm of maids occupied the room. Then more droves of workers flooded through a side door, and soon the clink of dishes and the busy chatter prevailed.

The dark-haired waiter who had served them all evening approached. "Do you need help with anything, sir? Ma'am?"

Fiona twisted her mouth to one side. "Thank you,

no. We were just waiting for everyone else to go."

The guy didn't seem sure what to make of that. He stood there, then turned on his heel, and strode away.

"I saw something." She stood. "Come on."

Tyler followed her. They stepped between maids balling up tablecloths and waiters scraping leftover desserts into buckets. Despite their obvious stares, no one stopped them. Tyler and Fiona reached the wall behind the Vanderbilt table where four recessed semicircles hosted white vases displaying red roses.

"These are nooks, right?" She poked her hand behind one of the containers.

Several of the workers eyed him. Some faces bore curiosity, others suspicion.

He leaned close to her ear. "No way are we going to be able to stick something in there and have no one notice."

No sooner had the words left his mouth than someone cleared his throat.

"Can I be of assistance, sir?" An older man with thinning hair stepped close to them and clasped his hands behind his back. His wrinkled features betrayed no emotion, but his eyes spoke a mixture of curiosity and reprimand.

"No thank you." Fiona waved him away.

The man didn't budge.

"My wife was admiring the flowers." Tyler took her elbow. "But we were just leaving."

They wove back through the dining area and out the way they'd come.

In the hallway, she jammed her hands on her hips. "How are we supposed to know where to put the book? A dozen or more places could be considered a nook. And besides, what does that have to do with two o'clock or dessert?"

Not having an answer, he rubbed a tight muscle in the back of his neck. He could figure this out. After all, he solved problems for a living. Sure, he had an engineer's license, but mostly he made decisions and fixed problems. And there was never a shortage of those.

But this situation fell outside his area of expertise. Scratch that. It fell outside the entire realm of believability. How could he find a solution when nothing made sense?

Lord, I need some help. I can't see an inch past my nose in this. But I know you can see us. See everything. Where do you want us to go now?

Fiona nibbled her bottom lip like she did when something troubled her.

He surveyed the floor, the walls, and the ceiling, hoping some kind of clue would jump out. His gaze slid past an adjacent doorway and then snapped back. What was that? From the corner of his eye, he'd seen something flicker.

There it was again. A glint of light like what happened when he caught the angle of the sun on a hand mirror.

He grabbed her fingers. "Let's look in there."

Hand in hand, they entered a storybook library. Mahogany shelves lined the walls with leather-bound volumes from floor to soaring ceiling. "Jackpot." He snapped his fingers. "What better place to hide a book than in a library?"

This had to be the right place. Besides, hadn't a glint of light in the fireplace led her to the book in the first place? He whispered an awed thanks to God, who, if he were being honest, Tyler hadn't expected to answer his prayer. At least, not in such an obvious way.

Can you do that at home sometimes? Might be helpful.

He somehow got the uncanny feeling God chuckled at him.

Fiona had paused just inside the doorway, her attention drawn to the ceiling-high shelves. He tucked his thumbs into his pockets. If he knew his wife at all, she was thinking about Belle and swinging from a ladder attached to the wall.

She puffed out a breath. "You know, I bet this is what Belle felt like when she found that castle library."

Tyler couldn't help his chortle. Right on cue.

She tugged her gaze from the books. "What?"

"Nothing. Just thinking about how cute you are."

Fiona rolled her eyes, but her cheeks tinged a pleased pink.

He pointed to the far wall, bringing them back to focus. "While you were gawking, I found something helpful. Look at that big map."

Her gaze dropped from the chandelier. "It's a map of America."

The drawing had to be at least five by six feet and included not only intricate topography details but also beautiful artistry with decorated edges and illustrated animals. Its gilded frame must've been custom-made.

"And look what's right underneath that clock up there." He moved to stand behind her, positioning her the right way.

A tingle of excitement sparked through him when she gasped.

"You're a genius!"

He didn't know about that. But he basked in the compliment all the same.

"Dessert at two. And this map has a clock hanging over Alaska. We had Baked Alaska for dessert." Her eyes widened. "Oh! Did you know that was invented at Delmonico's?"

Before he could say he hadn't and ask how she knew that factoid, she moved on. "But there's no nook. Just a map and a clock."

"Maybe we need to look closer."

They approached the console table under the map and scoured the area. Still no nook.

"Maybe it's more of a figurative thing," Fiona

mused. "We just need to stash it somewhere for the next person. However this whole thing works, the person who needs to will find it regardless, right?"

Made sense. "So where do you want to put it? There's a drawer in this table."

"I guess that's fine." She tugged open the drawer. "Hey, look. There's something in here."

She plucked out a sparkly object and handed it to him.

"Wow. Who would leave this in a random drawer?"

The bracelet in his palm had to be worth a fortune. Crusted in an intricate layer of diamonds, emeralds, and rubies, it could be on display at Buckingham Palace.

"We better put that back."

After closing the book and bracelet inside, she stepped back and sighed. "Is that it, then? Is this Cinderella's stroke of midnight? We've done everything, and this carriage is about to turn into a pumpkin?"

He wrapped her in a hug. "Mrs. Easley said we have the whole party. Now that we're done with the scavenger-hunt part, why don't we get back to dancing?"

She gave a nod but didn't move. "You think we will go back to the boys and our normal lives at dawn?"

He could only hope. But she didn't need to see his doubt. "Of course." He nodded toward the drawer. "Before we go, how about we say a little prayer like the notebook writer asked."

"Right." She stepped back and took both of his hands and bowed her head, waiting on him to lead.

He didn't mean to start by thanking God for his beautiful wife, for the life and love he had given them, or for the grand adventure he'd sent them on. But the words poured from Tyler's heart. Then they flowed from thanksgiving to petitions for protection.

"Lord, I ask that you send the traveler safely home. I don't know their story, but you do. You always know our story. I ask that you send us home at the end of this night to our boys, and I pray that we don't forget the lessons you have taught us here." He finished in Jesus's name, and Fiona echoed his amen.

When she looked up, she dabbed tears from her eyes. "Thanks, hon."

He kissed her forehead. Then they slipped out of the library and into the hallway.

From upstairs, the music beckoned.

Eighteen

Had any night ever been so perfect? Fiona ignored the strange looks she and Tyler received as they danced their own steps instead of following the carefully constructed choreography of the couples around them. Not that they knew any of those dances anyway.

And she didn't care a whit about what these people thought. She and her husband stayed at the edge of the room so they didn't disturb anyone and enjoyed one another's company. The music embraced her, the heady scent of his cologne tickled her senses, and contentment warmed her heart. Oh, how they'd needed this.

Tyler spun her around and then dipped her into a bend before guiding her upright once more.

"You know, I had no idea you were this good at dancing," she teased. "We've been married ten years. You've been holding out on me."

"Gotta keep you on your toes." He winked as they took another turn. "You'll think I'm boring if I don't store up surprises for you."

"I find you anything but boring. You are my favorite person on earth and the greatest blessing God's given me in this life."

Tyler slowed their steps and eased her closer, settling his hands on the curve of her waist. "That means the world to me, love. Thank you." They swayed before he continued, "I have to admit, at first I wasn't too keen on this unexpected feature of our trip. But I'm enjoying it more than I would have the weekend we had planned."

"Excuse me." A brusque male voice interrupted their conversation.

Fiona startled, and they stopped dancing. She expected to find another disgruntled elite to condemn them for their lack of social bearing.

Instead, a man dressed in a dark suit with his hat tucked beneath his arm stood about a foot away. Caught up in the moment, she mustn't have noticed his approach. The event, however, hadn't escaped the observant partygoers attempting to eavesdrop.

"Can we help you?" Tyler kept a protective arm around her waist.

"I need you both to come with me." The man nodded toward the doorway. "Quietly, if you please."

"What for?" Tyler's fingers tightened on her dress even as his voice remained calm.

"I have questions regarding your activities in the Vanderbilt residence." The man lowered his voice to a tight whisper. "I am an officer of the law, and Mr. Vanderbilt requested that I escort you to his study. Discreetly."

Fiona's heart fluttered as he punctuated the last word like a jab. Were they in some sort of trouble? "We have an invitation. We didn't crash the party."

The officer turned his blue gaze her way. "You'll have the opportunity to explain yourselves if you come with me now."

Did he imply they wouldn't have that opportunity if they didn't?

Tyler nudged her forward. "We haven't done anything wrong, so we don't mind answering your questions."

Despite his assurance, her nerves tingled. Why were they being questioned? Sure, some of the guests hadn't cared for them, but being beneath the others' perceived station was hardly a crime.

The officer guided them toward the doorway. Regardless of what he'd said about discretion, escorting people from the premises drew attention. Women whispered behind fans, many with catty expressions. Men looked down their noses. Fiona notched her chin high and ignored them all. These people's opinions didn't change who she was. Or the truth.

Of course, the truth was they came from the future and had gotten the invitation from what one could only say was a strange woman. Fiona would be suspicious of them too. They didn't belong. But they weren't guilty of anything, even if they had something to hide.

They endured the trip through the ballroom, down the stairs, and to the room across the hall from where she'd chased Mrs. Easley. They stepped into a masculine space replete with dark leather, paneled-wood walls, and heavy furniture. Only the faint smell of cigar smoke occupied the office.

The officer gestured to a couch near a wall of bookshelves. "You may sit, if you prefer."

"I'll stand." Tyler clasped his hands in front of him that way he did when he was preparing for the worst.

To that end, she chose to sit.

"Your names, please." The officer retrieved a notebook and pencil from his shirt pocket.

"Tyler and Fiona Robinson." Her husband cut her a look that said this could go off the rails.

Lord, help us.

"And where are you from?"

Tyler kept the man's gaze. "Mississippi."

"And what brings you to New York?"

"We had an invitation to this party tonight."

All truthful answers.

The officer scribbled the information. "May I see that invitation?"

Tyler shifted his feet. "I no longer have it."

Right. They'd left his jacket in the room with the fireplace.

"We didn't get your name," Tyler said as the man studied him and then wrote something else in the notebook.

"Clemmons."

"We also had places set at dinner, in case you are wondering," Tyler supplied. "We sat with Mr. and Mrs. Morris and Mr. and Mrs. Pembroke. You can ask them about our place cards."

Officer Clemmons arched a brow and then made another notation. "Would you kindly remove those masks?"

What was he writing?

Fiona tugged the strings loose and removed the plaster mask from her face and set it beside her on the couch. She placed Tyler's next to her own.

Judging by the man's frown and more scribbling, they hadn't done a great job at cleaning away the soot. How strange must they look?

"Were you on the premises earlier today and asked to leave?" Clemmons went back to the tiny notebook.

This time, she spoke up. "We went to the front, yes. But then the man at the door told us that the ball wasn't for several hours."

"And then did you take it upon yourselves to sneak through the servant's entrance and gain access to the house without permission?"

How did he know that? Had he already been questioning other people? She shifted her weight and tucked her fingers under her. Probably that butler.

"We did, yes," Tyler answered. "But only because we were helping with the flowers. That poor boy couldn't have carried that giant vase on his own."

The officer regarded him. "You, an invited guest, decided to assist a delivery boy?"

Tyler shrugged. "I saw him struggling."

A line formed between the man's blond brows. "What did you do after that?"

"We hired a coach, and I took my wife for dinner at Delmonico's. Then we returned here, showed our invitation at the door, and came to the party."

"I don't know where or how you obtained said invitation." Officer Clemmons maintained a flat tone. "But Mr. Vanderbilt claims he has never met you before and is certain you were not on his wife's list."

Fiona couldn't refute the claim. They could give no explanation that wouldn't label them as crazy.

Tyler scraped a hand through his hair. "It seems like there was some kind of miscommunication. Regardless, my wife and I do not want to cause any trouble, and it's getting late anyway. So we'll head back to our hotel."

"Which hotel is that?" The man readied his pencil.

"The Fifth Avenue."

The officer didn't even write it down. His lids hooded his eyes. "You two helped servants, then went to Delmonico's, and you have a room in the Fifth Avenue?"

"Yes." She and Tyler spoke in unison and shared a loaded look. The officer must find that list suspicious.

Clemmons widened his feet. "You, who are obviously not members of society, have a room at the Fifth Avenue and had a meal at Delmonico's."

His skepticism set Fiona's nerves on edge. Still, it seemed like a rhetorical question, so neither of them answered.

After more scribbling on his pad, the officer spoke again. "Some of the guests have reported missing jewelry. What do you know about that?"

Fiona's pulse tripped, and she sat back. "We don't know anything about missing jewelry."

"We didn't steal it, if that is what you are implying," Tyler said.

Officer Clemmons wrote in his notebook again.

"We didn't do anything wrong." Tyler stuffed his hands in his pirate trousers, his frustration evident in every taut line of his body. "We had an invitation and decided to enjoy the night together. Just because we aren't rich snobs doesn't mean we are thieves."

The officer's eyes narrowed. "Mr. Vanderbilt thinks otherwise. When one of his ilk seeks out a policeman on the street in the middle of an event like this, we take it seriously. A few of the ladies informed Mrs. Vanderbilt of their missing items."

"All we did was dance and go to dinner," Fiona countered.

"So you weren't seen"—he flipped to another page in his little book—"fleeing down the stairs and through the house and entering rooms that were not open to guests?"

"Well, I mean, yes, but there's an explanation for that." How that explanation would sound might be another matter.

"And Mr. Robinson was seen by several witnesses pushing Mrs. Pembroke down the steps. Her jeweled bracelet was discovered missing soon after."

"Wait." Tyler held up a finger. "I accidentally ran into her on the stairs. I didn't push her. And both she and her husband were at our table at dinner. She never said anything about a missing bracelet."

"We did find a bracelet in a drawer. I wonder if that was hers?" Oops. Fiona winced over her mumbled words.

Officer Clemmons scribbled something else. "What were you doing going through drawers in someone else's residence?"

Her stomach clenched. Drat. That sounded pretty bad.

"We shouldn't have done that." Tyler extended his palms. "But I promise we weren't stealing anything. You are welcome to search us. We haven't taken a thing."

"There will be time for that once we reach the station. For now, I have more questions."

"Station?" Fiona squeaked. "We can't go with you

to the station. We have to get home to our children."

The man leveled a cold gaze on her. "Then perhaps you should have thought about that prior to committing a crime."

Nineteen

This wasn't how he'd wanted to spend his anniversary. Tyler gripped Fiona's hand as the back door of the barred carriage slammed shut. People still lining the streets had craned their necks to watch Officer Clemmons escort them out of the Vanderbilt mansion into the waiting Victorian jail transport.

"You'd have figured some of these people would've gone home by now." Fiona huffed. She crossed her arms over her chest and settled her back on the wooden wall.

The matching bench underneath them provided little comfort.

The door opened again, and two men were shoved inside, both reeking of liquor. Tyler wrapped his arm around his wife and nestled her into the corner as far away from the cursing men as possible.

Nope. Not at all how he'd expected to spend his anniversary.

After some more shouting outside, one more man

entered the tight confines. Rail-thin with what looked like a historical version of a mechanic's coveralls hanging from his frame, he turned wide, confused eyes on Tyler.

Someone banged on the sidewall, and the vehicle lurched into motion. One of the larger two men made a retching sound.

"Oh no," Fiona started. "He's not going to—"

The stomach-churning stench of stale alcohol mixed with bile had Tyler gagging. Fiona covered her nose with her hand and closed her eyes. He offered her his sleeve while he tugged the neck of his loose cotton shirt up to his eyes.

A few blocks later, they were blessedly released from the hothouse of stench. He leaped over the mess in the rear and then helped Fiona. When she lifted her hem and jumped, he caught her around her waist and steadied her on the ground.

"Get moving." An officer they hadn't seen before motioned with a club toward a stone building.

Keeping one arm wrapped around Fiona, Tyler led them up a set of steps. Behind them, the officers dealt with the two drunk men. The lean guy yelled something about "besting the coppers" and tried to make a run for it. He'd gained less than ten feet before they had him in handcuffs.

Tyler opened the police station door to an entry room with stone floors, plain walls lined with empty benches, and a desk manned by an elderly officer.

Officer Clemmons motioned them toward a back door. "Mrs. Robinson, you'll go that way. Mr. Robinson, you'll come with me."

Tyler's grip on Fiona tightened. "I don't want to be separated from my wife."

"We don't have any females present to conduct a search, so I thought it best to allow Mrs. Robinson some privacy." Officer Clemmons stepped through the door. "This way, please. Mrs. Robinson, you will strip down and leave every item of your clothing by the door so one of my men might retrieve it and search for any stolen items."

Fiona's face went pale.

Tyler's pulse flared. "She will do no such thing!"

Clemmons passed where they stalled in the hallway and continued to another door a few steps down.

"There will be a robe in the room for you to cover yourself with, ma'am." The officer ignored Tyler. "Leave your hair down so the officer might see you've concealed nothing in there. If these terms are unacceptable, I can place you in the women's holding area until morning when someone is available to complete the search."

He pulled a key ring from his pocket and flipped through the keys.

Fiona clutched Tyler's arm. "I don't want to spend the rest of the night in a Victorian jail."

When her voice pitched a notch too high, the officer cut her a sidelong glance. He found the right key, slid it into the lock, and clinked it open.

As much as Tyler wanted to spare her any of this, what choice did they have? Maybe if they submitted to the search, they could prove their innocence and leave. The search, with stipulations, of course, would be better than going into holding. They would be separated and who knew if that would affect their return passage.

The thought dropped a weight into his stomach. What if they had to be inside the Vanderbilt house to go home? The sooner they got out of here the better.

"I demand to see no one else is in the room first." Tyler rubbed a circle on Fiona's back to reassure her. "And I'm not leaving from outside this door until my wife is allowed to dress again."

The officer opened the door and did something inside. Soon a soft glow emanated from within. He lingered and regarded Tyler. After several heartbeats, he nodded, widened the opening, and edged aside for Tyler to inspect it.

No bigger than a closet, the only thing in the space was a wooden bench topped with a folded black robe. Next to the door, a gaslight with a copper disc hung on the wall and provided flickering light.

Gripping Fiona's shoulders, he rotated her to face him. The censure in her gaze undid him. "You don't have to do this."

She hesitated. Then determination hardened her features. "But it's better than the alternative. I'll be fast. I have nothing to hide."

That last part, spoken more loudly than the rest, was for the officer's benefit.

Tyler squeezed her shoulders. "I'll be right here the whole time."

With a brave nod, she disappeared into the room. He waited with his arms crossed until the door opened again. She stood wearing a monk-style sack robe devoid of pockets or even a collar. Her curly red hair hung in disarray around her shoulders.

"Step back, sir." Officer Clemmons entered and retrieved Fiona's clothing before checking every inch of the room.

Tyler moved to the side enough for the officer to exit with the bundled gown. She'd even included her shoes.

She turned in a tight circle. "See? Nothing to hide."

Officer Clemmons called for another man by the name of Peters, and a portly fellow with a bushy mustache appeared through the door behind them.

"Search these." Officer Clemmons thrust the bundle toward him.

Peters checked every inch of Fiona's dress and then handed it and her shoes back. He slipped away again without a word.

"Shake your hair out," Officer Clemmons instructed.

Fiona flipped her hair over the man's boots and shook the curls with both hands.

Shocked, he stumbled a half step back before regaining his composure.

With a defiant glare, she tossed her hair over her shoulders and raised both arms, exposing her wrists and elbows.

"See? Nothing there, either. Next, are you going to ask me to hike up my hem and show you my knees?" She lifted the edge of the robe, revealing her soot-covered feet.

Officer Clemmons's cheeks puffed out, and he made the oddest blustering noise—like when a horse blew a breath out of their lips with a rumbling sound.

Despite the situation, Tyler had to hold a smirk in check. His wife was a feisty one.

"Thank you, ma'am. That is quite enough." Officer Clemmons handed the clothes back to her without meeting her eyes. "You may dress."

She snatched the bundle and closed the door with more force than necessary. The officer cleared his throat and tugged on his lapels until Fiona emerged wearing the rumpled white dress that exposed her arms. Her hair still hung around her shoulders, which seemed to make the policeman uncomfortable.

Served him right. He'd done plenty to make the two of them uncomfortable.

Clemmons called for Peters again, and the silent

man reemerged.

"Watch her while I search this one." Clemmons jerked his thumb toward Tyler.

"Not a chance." Tyler held up his hand. "I am not leaving my wife with some strange man while you make me go undress."

Officer Clemmons's lips compressed into a line. He cut a glance to Fiona's glare, then grunted. "Very well. She may attend us while I search you. But she must stay out of distance for you to attempt to hand her anything."

"We've got nothing to hide."

They entered the room, and the officer motioned Fiona to the corner. "Wait there, please."

With an eye roll, she put her back against the wall and pressed her lips tight.

Tyler removed his shirt and shook it out and turned out both trouser pockets. Then the officer had him remove his tall boots and socks, leaving him in nothing more than the form-fitting pirate pants. Good thing, the man realized Tyler couldn't have stashed anything in there and allowed him to redress.

"Can we go now?" Tyler asked. "I told you we didn't steal anything."

"I have more interviews to conduct, and of course, we'll need to hold you until the missing items are found."

"Hold us?" His chest tightened. "With what probable cause? No. I want a lawyer."

Officer Clemmons's brows inched higher. "Do you have a lawyer in New York?"

"N–no." Tyler sputtered. "You can supply one for me."

The man's head drew back.

Fiona stepped closer and kept her voice low. "There aren't any Miranda rights yet."

Tyler clenched his fists. Of course not. They might not have any rights at all. They were at the mercy of the past.

Still, he couldn't accept defeat. He glared at the other man. "There are still rights under the Constitution. We can't be held without probable cause. This man has no evidence that we've done anything wrong. All he is going off is the fact that we didn't fit in with high-society snobs. Apparently, that makes us the only people under suspicion."

Hands on his hips, Officer Clemmons rocked back on his heels. "Mr. Robinson, given the amount of wealth of all those attending the ball—save your-selves—what reason would any of them have to become jewel thieves?"

His chest buzzed. Logical argument. "That doesn't mean we are to blame. You have no evidence. And anyone could be a thief, no matter their social status."

"Then you have no reason to fear waiting on jus-tice."

Before either of them could respond, the man turned on his heel and left the room. A second later, a lock slid into place.

Twenty

"How are we going to get out of here?" Fiona paced the drab space constricting her like an anaconda.

Tyler sank against the wall. "Maybe it won't matter. Maybe we'll just, I don't know"—he snapped his fingers—"poof right out of here."

Bless him for feigning confidence, but she wasn't fooled. He didn't believe that either. "What if we have to be in the house? Or we were supposed to meet Mrs. Easley again? What if we put the book in the wrong place and now we are the adventurers who despair, lost in the past and all that? It's got to be nearing dawn by now."

"Why don't you come sit by me?" He patted the hard bench.

Fatigue weighted her every muscle, but her internal fluttering refused to let her be still. He patted the bench again. Exhaling, she settled next to him. When he wrapped an arm around her middle and snugged her close, her body relaxed, and she rested her head on his shoulder.

"Worrying ourselves to death won't change anything." His smooth voice further unwound her nerves. "We can pray, we can wait, and we can hope. But if I've learned one thing during this crazy night, it's that worrying over things I can't control isn't going to solve the problem."

She huffed an exhausted chuckle. "Remember that next time you're agonizing over work issues that are out of your hands."

He grew quiet.

"Sorry." She took his hand. "I thought that would come out as teasing or a joke, but it came out snide. You're right about all the worrying."

Before he could answer, the lock scraped and the door opened. An officer they hadn't seen before appeared. This man must be from the day shift. His alert brown eyes regarded them from a masculine face that didn't carry the weight of a night corralling the historical version of celebrity paparazzi and fans.

"Mr. Robinson, come with me."

Tyler stiffened. "I'm not leaving my wife."

The officer unhooked a pair of handcuffs from his belt. "You don't have that option."

"Why?" Fiona gripped Tyler's hand. "What's happened?"

The officer stepped farther inside the room. Two

other men appeared in the doorway.

"Where is Officer Clemmons?" Tyler rose as the man approached.

"Hands behind your back, Mr. Robinson. Let's not make this more difficult than it needs to be."

Fiona stood by Tyler, a vise grip on his arm. "Where are you taking him?"

"Holding."

The man grasped Tyler's other elbow, and Tyler tensed.

"Mrs. Robinson." The officer's voice iced over her. "Release your husband and step back. You will be moved to the female holding area."

"You can't put us in jail without a trial." Tyler clenched his fists. "I want to speak to a lawyer."

"If you have one you can contact in the city, the allowance will be made for you to do so." The officer secured both hands behind Tyler's back and snapped the cuffs into place.

Tyler's worried gaze slammed into hers.

"Wait." Her stomach plummeted. "What about our phone call? Don't we get one of those?"

The officer gave her a strange look.

She sucked a long breath through her nose and released it through her dry lips. "I mean, we get to contact someone about us being in here, don't we?"

"Let Officer Nicks know who you wish to contact." The man shuffled Tyler out of the door. The latch clicked behind them.

Her heart thudded. This couldn't be happening. It had to be a nightmare. Had to be!

Lord! You promised we would go home. You can't leave us here like this.

No sense of peace overcame her. Instead, her fears magnified until they nearly choked her. She pounded on the locked door. "Hey!"

At least three minutes of shouting and a sore fist later, the lock rattled. Fiona stepped back.

The door swung open, and an unpleasant fiftyish woman regarded her with pinched lips and judging brown eyes. "You there. Stop all this caterwauling."

"Please." Words burst out. "They took my husband, they won't tell me anything, and I was supposed to get a chance to tell someone I'm in here. I have children. We need to get home to our children."

The woman in a starched brown dress watched her with a bland stare. "I'm to report to Officer Nicks the person whom you wish to contact."

"Her name is Mrs. Easley."

"Residence?"

Fear tripped through Fiona's chest. "Um, I don't know. She may still be at the Vanderbilt residence."

The thin-faced woman's expression soured. "We will *not* be contacting any of your accomplices."

"Accomplice?" Fiona raised both hands. "No. You don't understand. We didn't steal anything."

"Yet we have numerous reports of a sword-wielding pirate and his female companion causing disturbances, bumping into guests who later were missing jewelry, and repeated sightings of you two running from staff members seeking to remove you from the premises."

"There's an explanation for that. And it wasn't thievery." Her hands flopped to her sides. "Mrs. Easley can explain everything. She gave us the invitation."

A glint sparked in the woman's eye. "So you admit you did not acquire a proper invitation."

"That's not what I said. Just that she was the one who gave it to us. The invitation had our names on it. We had places at dinner." Fiona twisted her fingers together. "We were supposed to be there."

"So you say." The woman crossed her arms over her thin chest. "If you do not have someone of repute to assist you, then you will have to wait until the investigation concludes."

"But—"

The door slammed on her protest.

Fiona sank onto the bench and put her head in her hands. How had this all gone so wrong?

Tyler gripped the cold metal bars and tried to calm his pounding heart. Morning light slithered through the grimy window and over the gaggle of unwashed men in the holding cell.

Morning light.

His knuckles whitened. Dawn should have been their stroke of midnight. When the carriage went back to a pumpkin. When the fairy-tale night ended. They should have been transported home.

Had they done something wrong with the scavenger hunt or put the book in the wrong place like Fiona had said?

The cool, damp air permeating the musty space did nothing to stop the sweat spreading across his shoulders. What would happen to their boys if they didn't get home? He closed his eyes and propped his forehead on the bars.

I don't know what to do, God. We need your help.

Movement to his left drew his attention, but he ignored the shuffling feet.

I thought you sent us on this adventure. Why would you abandon us?

Someone cleared their throat, and Tyler pried his tired eyes open to find the weird guy from the jail carriage staring at him. The thin older man who had tried to escape.

"Anyone coming for you?" The man glanced at the other prisoners and kept his voice low.

"No one knows I'm here except my wife who's here with me," Tyler replied, unable to keep the bitter bite out of his tone.

The man shrugged. "Same. Well, the part about nobody knowin' I'm in here." He stuck out a hand. "Eustis Cavanaugh."

Tyler pried his fingers from the bar and accepted the man's calloused grip. "Tyler Robinson."

After two pumps, the man kept his hold. "You're not from here, are you?"

"No." Tyler plucked his fingers free. "You?"

Hazel eyes bore into him. "You could say that. At least, not from *this* city."

A tingle rose along Tyler's neck, and he looked closer at the man's outfit. He hadn't seen anyone else wearing anything similar. "What do you mean by that?"

One of the men shifted behind them and coughed. The bigger fellow next to him cursed the other's foul breath and shoved him. The first man tumbled into the next man on the bench. Tyler ignored their cursing. Then they settled down and slipped back into grunts and snores.

Eustis sucked on his teeth. "Let's say the city's changed, is all."

"Changed since when?" Tyler studied the other man. Something about the way he spoke… "What are you hinting at, Eustis?"

The man returned Tyler's scrutiny. "I get the feeling you might know."

Tyler released a long breath. He was seeing things

that didn't exist. This man didn't know anything about time travel. Why would he? He was just some homeless guy off his rocker. Tyler closed his eyes and rested his head on the bars again. He needed to think.

"See, I was on the work crew to demolish this old house for that new Hickson site," Eustis said, his words laden with meaning. When Tyler didn't respond, he nodded with his chin toward the pirate shirt.

"Factory made, I'd say. Stitching is too even. Different from what the rest of these blokes have, eh?"

Tyler's knuckles whitened. The word choices. Maybe this guy *wasn't* from this time.

Before he could work out the words to ask, Eustis barked a chuckle. "Thought so. Like I said, we was getting ready to tear down that old house. Found this book, and next thing I know..."

Tyler's heart pitched toward his throat.

"Looks like you do know something about that after all, eh?" Eustis splayed his fingers. "Suddenly that old house wasn't so old anymore, and these fancy folk were everywhere. Some kind of party and horses and carriages like don't nobody but them way out in the country got no more."

"Where's the book? Do you have it?" Tyler leaned close. He did his best to keep his voice down, but one of the men stirred.

Eustis turned his palms out. "Coppers took it. I tried to make a break for it, but they snagged me and tossed me in here."

"When was that?" Tyler asked.

Eustis tilted his head. "About the same time, they pulled you from that fancy party."

Tyler's pulse thundered in his ears. If he had the book, then... "When, exactly, did you start work on that old house?"

Eustis raised his eyebrows. "You won't believe me."

"Try me."

They stared at one another for a solid count of three before Eustis whispered, "Nineteen... twenty-seven."

Tyler reeled back. This guy? He'd been a guest at The Depot? No, he'd been on a New York construction crew. But that didn't make sense. Tyler shook the questions away. None of that mattered.

Maybe they could help each other. "We have to get that book back."

A slow grin pulled Eustis's lips from yellowed teeth. "You don't sound surprised, and you even look like you believe me. No one else I tried to tell did. All them coppers said I was mad and should be hauled to the nuthouse. But not you. Only one reason for that, see. What's your year?"

Inexplicably, caution warned him against specifics. "Let's say you could be my great-grandfather."

Eustis let out a long whistle. "I knew it. That house's got some kind of witchcraft. Should have burned it when I had the chance."

Goose bumps flared along Tyler's skin. "How did you"—he glanced at the other prisoners, but none of the other four seemed to be listening—"make the jump?"

"Saw this fellow darting out of the house with a book in his hand. Looked funny. The man, see. Not the book. Don't care much for reading. He was wearing these strange clothes like nothing I'd ever seen. Shiny like. Looked like he was trying to escape with something valuable from the looks of 'em and weren't nobody supposed to be in that house noways. I grabbed him, and everything went black. When I woke up, it was dark out, and there were horses and carriages everywhere."

Earlier he'd said he'd found the book. Now his story changed. "And the book?"

The glint returned to Eustis's eye. "Like I said. Lost it."

"Where did the other guy get it?" Tyler raked a hand through his sweaty hair.

"How should I know?"

Tyler withheld a groan. Had the other man been the real time traveler, and Eustis had gotten sucked in by mistake? Maybe the other man had been at Mrs. Easley's inn at some point as well. Tyler hoped the traveler made it home. And he could only pray that Eustis taking the book from the Vanderbilt house hadn't disrupted the time loop. What if that was why they didn't go back at dawn?

Eustis leaned against the bars and picked his teeth with his thumbnail. "Good riddance to that bit of witchery, I say. I'm not going back nohow."

"Why?"

"Been thinking about it. Fresh start here. No debts. No cronies lookin' for me."

"I have two sons." Tyler swallowed against a sudden lump of emotion. "I must get home to them."

Eustis clapped him on the shoulder. "That so? Who am I to stop a man who wants to make a decent pa outta himself, eh?" He offered a wry chuckle. "Good thing for you I can help. We'll have you back to them young'uns in no time."

Tyler could only stare as hope and caution wrestled within him. Could he trust this slippery guy to get him home?

Twenty-One

*H*uddled in the corner of the cold cell, Fiona pulled her knees to her chest. Her thin embroidered dress did little to ward off the chill. Earlier that morning, three other women had occupied the space with her, providing a modicum of body heat. But family members came to collect each of them hours ago.

Two had been sisters who'd gotten involved in a scuffle over the best viewing place on Fifth Avenue to see the Vanderbilt guests arrive, and the other had been a young woman whose clothing had marked her as one of the high-society types. Well, maybe midlevel society, seeing as how she didn't wear a costume like the guests.

Who knew what landed her in here. The blonde had sat on the bench with perfect rigid posture and never moved or spoke until a stoic older woman appeared and took her away without a word. The officers held the "disorderly" gawkers long enough for someone to come to collect them.

Now Fiona was alone.

She'd tried praying, but the words continued in a cycle without end. She longed to see Tyler. She needed to go home. She wanted to trust God's plan and timing, but worry continued to claw at her heart.

I want to believe and trust you, Lord. Please give me the strength to do so, because I don't think I can do even that on my own.

She sat in silence, focusing on being still and doing her best to ignore the hard bench, the cold wall, and the faint sounds of men talking in another room. After a time, parts of several verses settled into a peaceful response that warmed her spirit.

My grace is sufficient for you. Abide in me. Lean not on your own understanding, and I will direct your paths.

Comforted by the blanket of peace, she curled into a ball on the bench and drifted to sleep.

She awoke sometime later to shouts coming from down the hallway. Men's voices rose in a clamor and mingled into a distorted mess. She pressed her face against the cold bars, but couldn't see anything down the hall.

A door opened, and a stocky man with a kind face and a shock of graying hair bustled over.

"Hello, Mrs. Robinson. You're being released now."

Relief surged through her with such force that her knees softened and she gripped the bars to remain upright. Metal scraping through the lock had to be the best music ever played.

When the door opened, she surged through. "Thank you. I thought I might be in here forever. Thank goodness this mess is cleared, and we can go. Where's my husband?"

The guy in the pressed uniform only motioned her through the doorway and back to the main entrance where they'd arrived last night. A different man sat at the wooden desk by the wall. His dark gaze followed her before he bent over a book on the desk and made a notation.

The officer held open the front door for her. "Have a pleasant day, ma'am."

Fiona balked. "Where's my husband?"

"Mr. Robinson? We are still waiting for testimony before his release."

"But you're letting me go?"

The man's bushy eyebrows rose toward his receding hairline. "You'd rather stay?"

"Of course not." She clutched the front of her dress. "I want my husband to be released with me. You've realized we are innocent. Otherwise, you wouldn't be letting me go. So why release me and not him?"

"Mr. Robinson had the encounter with Mrs. Pembroke, and we are still waiting on more information from Mr. Pembroke, who has cast suspicion on Mr. Robinson." He scratched his chin and motioned toward the doorway. "There's a possibility for two thieves, but we cannot yet be sure until the final missing item is located."

"Wait. You said two, which means you have found the real thief."

The man's annoyed look said he wouldn't comment on that further.

Realization pulsed through her. Of course. Mrs. Pembroke and the missing bracelet. And Mr. Pembroke didn't care for Tyler at all, given the incident on the stairs.

"Would the missing item be a jewel-encrusted bracelet?" At the glimmer in the officer's eyes, Fiona continued. "It's in the drawer under the map in the library. I told Officer Clemmons that when we were still in the house. We found it there and put it back. We shouldn't have been snooping in the house, I know. But tell the officers to look there and take that bracelet to Mr. Pembroke. Then you'll see my husband is innocent."

Or make them further suspect she and Tyler stole it and stashed it there. She could only pray her attempt at cooperation and the truth would win out.

She twisted her hands together and waited. A grunt his only response, he thrust his chin toward the door.

"You are welcome to check back tomorrow." His tone, though friendly, left no more room for argument.

She stepped outside into a sunny day. Carriages crunched down the brick-paved streets, pedestrians strolled past, and conversations drifted on air carrying the scents of woodsmoke, horses, and baking bread.

The latter made her stomach knot.

Best she could tell from the position of the sun, it appeared to be mid to late afternoon. They'd left on Friday night, their time. Which should have made this Saturday. But she'd discovered the ball had been held on a Monday rather than a weekend. When you were that rich, you didn't have to worry about work the next day. Anyway, that made today in this time Tuesday.

Though knowing the day made no difference, she took satisfaction in gathering her bearings.

People flowed around her, creating an island of solitude. Dressed in tailored clothing topped with dismissive expressions, not a one offered more than to skirt past her.

"You don't belong here," each upturned nose seemed to say.

Fiona clutched her arms around her middle as a cold gust of air knifed through her flimsy dress. She couldn't see Tyler until tomorrow. So what was she supposed to do now?

Could she return to the Fifth Avenue Hotel room they'd woken up in? Maybe she could find some comfort there until they released Tyler. She couldn't return to the Vanderbilt house and look for the book or a way to teleport out of here. Even if they did let her in, she wouldn't try to time travel home without him.

The hotel, then. Plan in place, she still hesitated. Maybe the Vanderbilt butler would be nice enough to return Tyler's jacket and the outer layer of her dress. Walking around in that had been bad enough. Wearing nothing more than the thin white layer underneath—spotted with ashes, no less—made people even more wary of her.

And she needed money. Even if she did have a room at the hotel, she'd need to find something to eat. They had some of the cash Mrs. Easley had given them in Tyler's wallet. Was it still in his jacket? She couldn't remember. Another thought pushed aside the others.

What if they didn't feed Tyler? She'd need to bring him something. They wouldn't deny her that, would they?

She'd go to the Vanderbilt house, get their money, and then go to the hotel. She'd clean up there and then find somewhere to buy food. After taking supper to Tyler, she'd go back to the hotel for the night.

Beyond that, she had no idea. But at least she could see her next steps.

With her chin held high, she marched away from the police station. Block after block, she continued to Fifth Avenue. She traveled past stately houses and soaring mansions until she returned to the one that contrasted from the others. The limestone shone in the spring sunlight, a spot of white lace on an otherwise drab brownstone gown.

She approached the door and knocked. When a woman in a starched, blue high-necked dress topped with a white apron and matching cap opened the door, she took in Fiona's appearance with nothing more than curiosity. At least she didn't look down on her like that horrid butler. Fiona didn't know if she could take one more snotty person acting like she was something to scrape from their shoe.

"I'm sorry to bother you," Fiona said. "My husband and I attended the party last night, and my husband left his jacket in the parlor. Is it possible for you to check and see? It would be a deep-blue pirate jacket." Her face heated, but she pushed the next words out. "And the rest of my dress too. It's a coppery-brown fabric with floral brocade and puffed sleeves."

The woman shifted and glanced behind her.

Before she could refuse, Fiona added, "I'll wait outside of course, so as not to trouble anyone. If you would be so kind, it would mean a lot to me."

The woman hesitated, then nodded. "I'll return presently."

The door closed with a click, and Fiona positioned herself against the wall and as out of sight as she could manage on a busy street. Five minutes turned to ten and then what had to be thirty.

Maybe the woman had forgotten her. Should she knock and try again or give up and hurry to the hotel before it got late?

Oh no. What if returning here for these items made the police think she was smuggling something out of the house? Could the maid be talking to them now? Would they arrest her again? She took a step back. She'd have to forgo getting the money and—

The door swung open, and the woman emerged, carrying dark-blue and copper material.

"Oh! You found them. Thank you so much." Fiona reached for the garments.

"Good day, ma'am." She closed the door as soon as the fabric left her fingers.

Fiona pulled her embroidered dress on and then covered it with Tyler's heavier jacket for protection against the cool breeze. Then she tucked her hand inside the inner pockets. Both masks had been lost, but the wallet and Mrs. Easley's letter remained.

Relief weakened her muscles.

She opened the letter first to see if it contained any new information, but nothing had changed. If she ever made it home, she was going to have a talk with that woman about truthfulness and expectations. Home at dawn the next morning her foot! She returned the letter to Tyler's pocket and opened the wallet. Four dollars remained. They'd spent eight on supper and then three dollars for their trips in the hired carriage.

Not much by the normal standards, but here, it should get them something to eat tonight at least. Her tired feet begged for a ride in another hired hackney, but she had to conserve her money. It might take another day or more before they released him. She didn't know much about the current legal and jail systems, let alone that of New York in the 1880s.

Heaving a sigh, she started down the street toward the police station and, past that, the hotel where they'd started this wild experience. What felt like an hour later, she approached the Fifth Avenue Hotel. Thank goodness. Her feet and her back ached, and her throat and mouth felt stuffed with wool. When had she last had something to drink?

She hurried toward the swanky hotel's front door and nearly ran into a man dressed in a dark suit who had moved to block her path.

Fiona huffed. "Excuse me."

"May I help you?" The man scraped a gaze over her.

Fire leapt through her veins. "Oh no you don't. Don't you dare start that with me. I know I look a mess. I am aware my outfit is ridiculous and dirty. But so help me, you better get out of my way. I have a room here, and you are *not* going to stop me from returning to it."

The man drew his head back. "You have a room here?"

"Of course I do. What? You think just because a woman has had a difficult time and isn't looking her best she couldn't possibly have stepped foot in your pretentious establishment?" She jammed her hands on her hips and spoke through her teeth the way her grandmother always had when she'd been spitting mad. "Get out of my way."

The man sputtered something incoherent.

With a growl, Fiona reached around him and yanked the door open. He lurched out of her way as she stalked inside. People turned to stare, but she marched over marble floors and toward the staircase.

She made it as far as the first step before someone gripped her arm.

"Miss! You can't go to the guest rooms."

She snatched her arm from the skinny man holding her. "I can if I'm occupying one of those rooms."

The man pinched his lips together before he spoke. "*You* have a room? Under which name?"

"Robinson."

A line formed between his brows.

"It's on the second floor. I can take you right to it." Did she have anything inside to prove she'd been here before? Cold dread pooled in her center, but she refused to acknowledge it. She couldn't show any smidgen of doubt now.

"And your key?"

Her mind reeled. Had they had a key? They'd woken up in that room. Talked to the maid. Discovered they were in the past. But never had a key.

She patted Tyler's jacket pockets. It had to be here somewhere, didn't it?

The man gripped her elbow again. "If you'll come

with me, please."

"No!" She snatched free. "I have a room here, and I intend to stay in it until I can get my husband out of—" She snapped her teeth together before the word *jail* could come free.

"You said your name was Robinson, did you not?"

She glared at his fingers on her arm until he released her.

"There's a note at the front desk. It could be for you."

Something from Mrs. Easley? Fiona let out a breath and pulled her shoulders back. "You can deliver it up to my room."

The man shook his head. "There's no room booked for Robinson. Only the letter."

She swallowed and glanced up the stairs. She could make a run for it, but what good would that do? She couldn't break into a hotel room and barricade herself inside.

Fighting tears of wretched defeat, she followed the man to the lobby desk. She gripped the sides of Tyler's jacket until her fingers ached.

The thin man rummaged behind the desk and palmed a sealed envelope. "If you'll kindly take this and go so as not to disturb our patrons, we would appreciate your cooperation."

The back of her eyes burned as she took the letter with quaking fingers. She would not cry. Would not.

Judgmental gazes followed her across the shined floors, through the arched doorway, and out onto the wind-chilled street. Her insides melted into dismay.

She wrapped Tyler's jacket tighter around her shoulders and breathed in the faint scent of him. Never again would she take for granted his love for her or the fact that he came back to her every evening. Even if she had to take up residence in the police station, she'd be there waiting for him.

She'd argue for his release. Pay bail. Something. There had to be *something*.

Daylight faded, and shadows stretched long. Her feet plodded back toward the police station. What she wouldn't give to be home with Tyler and the boys in their cozy, messy house. Tears streaked down her cheeks as she wove through the crowds. Women in sculpted dresses and men in top hats. Carriages with horses. So foreign when all she wanted was her home tucked in their quiet neighborhood. To sit on her back porch and watch her boys play in the yard. To kiss her husband when he came home from work.

This adventure had lost its shine, and she needed a set of ruby slippers to send her home.

She reached the police station and dropped her tired frame onto the front steps. The letter contained a red seal pressed with the letter E.

Mrs. Easley. What would the woman say now? That they'd failed? They were stuck in the past? She wouldn't accept it. She slid her finger under the seal and opened the page.

She scanned the single line—Congratulations! Adventure complete.

Her vision grew dark around the edges, and her stomach lurched into her throat.

No!

She couldn't be leaving. Not without Tyler!

Desperate, she ripped the paper in half. Her head still swam. The darkness closed in.

Please! No! Don't take…me…away…from…

Everything faded as she slumped to the unforgiving ground.…

Twenty-Two

Shouts trampled the tenuous peace and jarred Tyler from his fitful dozing. This had to be the tenth time his cellmates erupted into an argument. He pried his crusty eyes open. Mere feet away, two men stood nose-to-nose, shouting about respecting the other's space—only in not-so-polite terms. Tuning them out, he shifted his weight to reposition his back against the cold wall. At least he'd claimed the corner end of the bench. The combination of back and shoulder support made attempting to sleep easier.

The men continued to debase one another, and he closed his eyes.

Each new man thrown into the cell had brought another layer of disruption, and even as others had filed out, new ones with equally turbulent manners replaced them.

Now it was Sunday morning. Or should be, at least on his timeline. He'd started to lose track. He was supposed to have returned to the Ocean Springs inn at dawn on Saturday morning, but an entire day and another night had passed since they were supposed to have gone home. There'd been no word from Fiona. Every waking moment he stewed over how she was holding up in the women's section. She had to be going mad with worry over their boys by now, same as him.

Something sharp poked into his side. "You awake?"

Tyler shifted to find Eustis staring at him. "Hard to sleep in these conditions."

"Look, I'm about to take a powder."

"What?" This man must be crazy. He couldn't intend to do drugs in here, could he?

The guy gave a derisive snort, the edges of his mouth a touch too hard to come across as friendly. "Don't you know nothin'? Means I'm about to scram out of this joint."

Tyler sat up straighter. Did someone post bail? He'd never said why they were holding him other than he'd got rounded up with the troublemakers outside the Vanderbilt ball.

As though sensing the unspoken question, Eustis lifted his chin. "Word in here is that after serving some time for disturbin' the peace, they let you out. So old Sticky E here is about to fly free." Eustis leaned close with a conspirator's whisper. "I should be able to get that book for you."

Tyler sat up straighter. "You know where it is?"

"Told you the coppers took it. Don't see why they

won't give it back to me." He cast Tyler a side-eye. "No promises."

"Thank you. That means—"

"In return, you'll do something for me, eh?"

Tyler pressed his lips together. "I don't have any money."

"I reckon you got something just as good." Eustis tapped his temple. "Smarts. Bet you know a fair bit more history than I do. Fellow can do well when he knows the future."

Did he mean like placing bets? On what? "I don't know much about the 1880s. I doubt I would be any help for whatever it is you are looking to do."

"We'll see." He slapped Tyler's shoulder. "You give me what I want, and I'll give you what you want. Fair trade."

"I want to go home." Tyler crossed his arms. "I'll never take my wife's supper waiting on me for granted again." His stomach rumbled in agreement.

They'd given the men some kind of thin oatmeal and water but not much to be sustained on. Seemed like everyone but him came through this room in short stints.

The other man made a strange half snort, half laugh. "If I get the book, then you can go back. But you'll repay my kindness first."

He didn't like the sound of that.

"What else are you going to do?" Eustis scoffed. "If

that book is the only way to travel like you and me traveled"—he leaned in close, his breath pungent, his words loaded—"then I'm your only hope."

Hope.

The word thrummed through him.

My hope is in the Lord.

"Actually, I'm good." Tyler shook his head. "The Lord got me out here. He can get me home. I'll wait and do it his way." If nothing else, he'd learned to quit trying to control everything.

Eustis cracked a snide laugh. "Didn't know you were one of those religious nuts."

Metal cracked on metal and startled the cacophony into stunned quiet. A hefty officer rapped his club on the cell bars again for good measure.

"Settle down, men!" When the grumbling subsided, he pointed to Eustis. "You. You're free to go."

Eustis waggled his eyebrows. "Last chance. We got a deal?"

Tyler almost wanted to agree. To make a plan. To do *something*. Anything to take matters into his own hands rather than sitting around and waiting while his wife suffered and everyone in their own time panicked over them missing.

Instead, he chose faith. "No thanks."

Eustis rolled his neck. "Suit yerself. Shame to see another man leave his young'uns. But that's just how it goes, I guess."

Sourness gathered in Tyler's empty stomach.

The officer unlatched the door, and Eustis slipped through, not sparing a backward glance.

Tyler's pulse quickened. Had he given up his only chance to leave? What if they accused him of a crime he didn't commit and he ended up serving a sentence? What if he and Fiona had already missed their window to return to the present?

What if they never got to go back home?

He pulled a breath into his lungs, held it, and pushed it back out again. For likely the hundredth time in the past forty-eight hours, he threw a prayer heavenward for help and tried to stifle his doubts that God was listening.

Over the next hours, he attempted to focus on internal praise. Every time his mind insisted on turning to worry, he began another prayer that God would give him strength in weakness. One by one, his cellmates emptied out until only the blessing of silence remained.

As darkness chased out the remnants of the day, footsteps sounded down the hall.

Tyler rose and stretched his back, then moved toward the front of the cell. He wanted to make sure to catch the officer coming by. Maybe without all of the chaos of the other prisoners, he might be granted some kind of information on Fiona.

But the form that separated from the shadows didn't belong to one of the police officers. Tyler squinted against the gloom as the feminine form neared. With unhurried steps, the woman glided down the hallway in a fitted gown that flared at the bottom made of some kind of shiny pink material. Where did she get so many outfits?

Tyler shook the ridiculous question away and gripped the bars. He pressed his face against the metal. "Mrs. Easley?"

She came to a stop in front of the cell and clasped her hands together as she regarded him. "What are you doing in here, Mr. Robinson? I do believe I sent you to a party."

He clenched his jaw, and he had to force himself to relax the muscles to speak. "We were trying to follow your stupid riddles when we were accused of a crime and brought here."

"My goodness. Well, adventures are known to take twists and turns, I suppose." She waved a hand through the air. "But never mind that. I'm pleased to see you chose wisely. You could have attempted to take matters into your own hands." Her eyes sparkled. "Though there are blessings in waiting on the proper timing."

The words tumbled around in his brain, grasping to take hold. "You mean Eustis?"

"I find it is always best to wait for justice rather than trying to force it. Those dear officers did follow up on Fiona's suggestion to check the drawer and take that bracelet back to Mr. Pembroke."

Tyler gaped at her.

"And…" She held up a finger to stop him from asking any questions. "They have discovered one enterprising young woman whom they should now have in custody to be the true culprit. Seems that Miss Eleanor Gillman figured the guests wouldn't miss any of those jewels and might be too prideful to admit it for fear of a scandal against Mrs. Vanderbilt if they did."

Tyler blinked. So the police knew he and Fiona were innocent but still hadn't released them?

"She was one of the maids, you see," Mrs. Easley attempted to clarify. "As she served the guests, she relied on her nimble fingers to relieve them of their trinkets. She stashed them around the house, intending to collect them while cleaning the next morning. Turns out her father had made bad investments and she was trying to help right the matter."

She clicked her tongue. "Of course, taking on her own version of Robin Hood was not the way to go about it."

"So they know we are innocent," Tyler voiced. "Why haven't they released us?"

"They already released Fiona. It took longer for you, I'm afraid, on account of Mr. Pembroke and his grudge. It wasn't until they brought him the bracelet and Mrs. Pembroke admitted to remembering a brief encounter with Miss Gillman that they determined you could not be the culprit despite your mishap on the stairs."

Air left his nostrils in a rush. "Then where is Fiona?" She'd been alone in the city? Anything could have happened to her! His pulse tripped through his veins.

"Perfectly safe. Sleeping soundly."

Tyler worked through her meaning. "She's safe? Did she go home?" At her mock long-suffering look, he let out a breath. "If I would have tried to find the book with Eustis or if I had agreed for him to get the book and then I tried to use it on my own...would I have been stuck here?" He didn't want to fathom spending the rest of his life separated from her.

"You would have never been lost to history, Mr. Robinson. We are never lost, we who are held in God's hand. I told you from the beginning. Only the Conductor decides when the trip is complete. He may have given you chances to learn to trust him and his timing, but you were never in danger of not returning to your children." She pulled something from a bag he hadn't noticed she carried draped over one arm.

The book.

Relief pounded through his veins. "You have it! Can you use it now, or do we have to wait for the officers to release me? Do we even need the book? We came here without it."

With a beguiling tip of her eyebrows, Mrs. Easley gestured toward the bench. "Perhaps you should have a seat. I find that helps."

Tyler's vision started to darken. He hadn't even

touched the book yet. Wait. Had she said if Fiona had already gone home or...? No. She'd only said she was safe. His insides rebelled. "Wait! Fiona! Is she—" His head throbbed.

"Not to worry, dear..." Whatever else Mrs. Easley said faded into a muted hum.

Tyler struggled against the darkness tugging at his senses. He had to find Fiona.

Had to make sure...

Before he could finalize the thought, everything went black.

Twenty-Three

Birds twittered, their delightful song poking through the warm darkness shrouding Fiona. Blissful warmth. And softness. She snuggled deeper into the blankets. Her foot connected with something, and she wiggled her toes. The familiar feel of her husband's leg jolted awareness through her.

Her eyelids popped open.

Tyler's sleeping face lay only inches away. Relief poured through her, and she grabbed his cheeks with both hands and kissed his forehead, the bridge of his nose, and both eyelids.

He stirred underneath her touch and stretched. His eyes drifted open, and a lazy grin spread over his lips. "Mornin'."

They were back!

They were safe, and together and—wait!

Tyler didn't seem at all surprised to wake up here. She sat up and flung the covers off. She wore the pajamas she'd packed. The cute little pink set with flowered pants and a tank top she'd bought specifically for this trip. But she never remembered putting them on. The last thing she remembered was opening the letter from Mrs. Easley and sitting on the police station's front steps.

In New York. In 1883.

Had it all been a dream?

Tyler stretched beside her, looking none too concerned. There was *no way* she'd dreamed all of that. Sunlight poured through the window and splayed over the charming room they'd barely seen before disappearing through time. She remembered coming in. Finding the costumes. Going to the party. Every conversation, dance, and moment they'd shared. She'd tasted that caviar. Been hauled to jail. Every second remained with perfect clarity. Everything except what should have really happened. They'd come to this room at the inn and then…what? She racked her brain.

She didn't remember ever unpacking her bag. Or putting on these pajamas.

"Man, I don't think I'll ever take a decent mattress and central heat for granted again." Tyler's warm voice slid over her and sliced through her mounting panic. "Or maybe it's air-conditioning. It's warmer in Ocean Springs for sure."

Fiona's head popped from where she'd been scrutinizing her clothing. "Warmer than where?"

His forehead crumpled. "Um…" He twisted his lips

to the side. "New York?"

"Is that a question, or do you have a reason for saying that?" She pounced onto her knees and leaned close to him, looking for any hint of the truth in his eyes.

"Come on, Fi. There's no way that was a dream, right? We were in New York."

"Yes!" She sat back. "The ball. And jail. I thought…"

The emotions returned. The ache when she thought she might be losing her husband across an impossible expanse of time.

Tyler held her close. "Mrs. Easley came to the jail, and before I knew what was happening, I was slipping back. I didn't know if I was leaving you." His voice thickened, and he cleared his throat. "But then I woke up, and you were here next to me, sleeping peacefully just like she said you were. And I thought maybe I'd dreamed all of it. I stared at you for, like, an hour. Then I decided it didn't matter if I'd dreamed it or not."

"Because the adventure taught us things worth holding onto," she finished for him. "But I don't think it was a dream."

"Yeah, I figured when you acted super weird when you woke up."

She swatted him. "I was weirded out that you weren't acting all weird!"

A knock sounded.

They looked at one another until a familiar singsong voice permeated the door.

"Good morning, dears! I've brought your breakfast. And I have coffee!"

In only a split second, Tyler crossed the room. Fiona scrambled out of the bed and followed.

"You!" Tyler yanked open the door, revealing a smiling Mrs. Easley holding a silver tray.

"Yes, me, dear. This is my home." She bustled past them and into the room to deposit the tray on the writing desk. "Now, here's a pot of fresh coffee, my homemade biscuits, sausages, and strawberries. Do you want any jelly or honey?"

Fiona gaped at her.

"You sent us to the past, didn't you?" Tyler blurted. "And you were there. I didn't dream that."

"It was lovely, wasn't it? Such a treat for me to get to visit a hub like that. I haven't gotten to do that in years. They are a bit tricky, what with all the coming and going, but it was lovely to see old friends again. We don't often get to cross paths in our line of work."

"So you *were* there." The words left Fiona in a breathy rush. "It was all real."

"Of course." Mrs. Easley beamed. "All our adventures are real."

Tyler stepped away from the door. "You said we would go home at dawn. You lied to us. I was in that jail for two days!" His face contorted. "What day is it?"

"Wait. You stayed two days?" Fiona asked. "But that doesn't make any sense. I went back on Tuesday. Well, the ball was on a Monday, but we left on Friday so the next morning was Saturday to us. Yes. I went back on Saturday evening." She pursed her lips. She'd figured they woke up here on Saturday morning as planned. Had they not?

Mrs. Easley ignored Fiona's confused jumble of words and smiled. "What time did you awake this morning?" Before Tyler could answer, she pointed to the window. "Were you not here to see dawn's light?"

"But you said dawn the night of the party," Fiona interjected. "You know, like Cinderella's midnight. Except, the next morning."

"Did I?" Mrs. Easley tapped her chin. "I seem to recall telling you that you wouldn't be gone any longer than you had planned to be and you would be back at dawn. And what do you know? Here you are, right on schedule."

"But we were… You made us think…" Fiona couldn't get her words to clarify her churning thoughts.

"I've found that time is a fairly relative thing." Mrs. Easley patted Fiona's shoulder like a doting grandmother. "Enjoy your breakfast."

"Wait." Tyler held up a hand. "What about the book? And Eustis?"

"Who is Eustis?" Fiona asked.

Mrs. Easley's brows gathered. "Do not be fooled,

for God is not mocked. That which a man sows, so shall he reap." At Tyler's confused look, she brushed a hand through the air. "The point is, no one gets away with things like they think they do. He was never anywhere he wasn't supposed to be for a purpose."

Fiona would have to ask Tyler what he meant later. He'd already taken that strange answer in stride and launched into another question.

"How many people wrote in that book? Do they all come from you? Or do other places like this suck unsuspecting people through time warps?"

Gentleness further softened Mrs. Easley's ageless face. "I don't have all the answers. Some things remain a mystery until we reach heaven. You and your wife went where you needed to go to learn what you needed to learn." She brightened and tipped her finger in the air like Fiona imagined a fifties' housewife might do in a commercial. "I am not the Conductor. I don't control the destination or the schedule. I'm only here to run the ticket booth."

"But I don't understand." Tyler rubbed at his temples. "If we were always going to end up here at dawn like you said, then what was all of that about despair and lost to time?"

"Would you not have despaired if you had not learned the lessons you were sent to learn? Would not the entire trip have been nothing more than something to be forgotten?" She splayed her fingers. "Lost to history?"

"English," Tyler grumbled. "Poems and metaphors. I dislike vague metaphors."

Mrs. Easley offered him a wry grin that he returned. "Yet difficulty is how we grow."

Fiona shared a warm look with her husband, and he laughed.

The lessons they learned were ones she hoped they'd never forget. That they would never take one another for granted again. She grabbed the older woman into a hug. She smelled of sugar cookies. "Thank you. It was a grand adventure, but I am so glad to be home again."

Mrs. Easley beamed. "Perspective does us all good, child. Now, I must be going. I have a young chef for whom I need to prepare. I trust you two can keep yourselves occupied for the rest of the weekend, hmm?"

With a wink, she swept out of the room.

"So, it's still Saturday morning?" Tyler asked, his forehead rumpled.

Fiona was already fishing her phone from her suitcase. Half battery. She punched Mom's contact and put the phone on speaker. Mom answered on the third ring.

"My, aren't you up early?" The laughter in Mom's voice unwound the tension coiling in Fiona's stomach. "I figured you'd want to sleep in."

They were truly back in the right time, and Mom hadn't been panicking over them missing.

"How are the boys?" Tyler asked.

"Perfect as always, of course."

A little voice cried out in the background.

"Noah, you want to come talk to your momma and daddy?"

Tyler gripped Fiona's shoulders and kissed the top of her head.

"Nanna let me have chocolate for breakfast!" Noah shouted into the phone.

His triumph broke a laugh free from Fiona's chest. "She did, huh?"

Mom huffed. "Now before you get upset, it was yogurt."

Tyler faked a gag. "They make chocolate yogurt?"

"Well, they make yogurt with M&Ms."

"It's fine, Mom. Enjoy spoiling them."

"Thank you," Mom sang out. "It's more fun if I don't have to try to hide it from you."

Tyler laughed at her teasing. "Did they behave for you last night?"

"Of course. We watched movies, played in a blanket fort, built block towers, and told bedtime stories to Lamby and Rabbit before we all fell asleep on the floor."

"You slept on the floor?" She couldn't picture Mom sleeping on the carpet.

"Sure. That's where all the mattresses are in the fort."

Fiona shook her head. "Oh. Well, in that case."

"Me too!" Ethan piped up. "I gave Babbit choc–*it* too. He like choc–it."

"I bet he does. He's going to need a bath after all that chocolate too, huh?" Fiona asked.

"No. We takin' the truck. Nanna say I drive."

"You can't drive," Noah whined. "That's my truck. I drive!"

The argument over who got to steer the battery-powered ride-in truck they'd gotten for Christmas faded into the background as Mom took the phone away. "Don't worry. I have it all under control. Y'all have fun."

"Thanks, Mom." Fiona sighed out her joy. "This has been a good trip."

"It's just started," Mom countered, her cheer a soothing balm. "Enjoy your day. We'll talk tomorrow."

They said their goodbyes, and Fiona disconnected the call.

"So, do you want to stay, or are you ready to go home?" Tyler asked.

"Mom said they are fine. We should enjoy the rest of our weekend together."

He wrapped her in a hug. "And we even got extra time, thanks to a time warp."

Fiona snuggled closer into his embrace. "Gee, I wonder what we are going to do with all this free time...."

"I'm sure we can think of—" He cut short as his phone rang. His chest heaved with a sigh.

Fiona wiggled free of his arms and inspected the breakfast Mrs. Easley had brought, trying not to let disappointment take a bitter hold.

"Is this an emergency?" Tyler asked the caller. Since the construction crews often worked on Saturdays, weekend calls were the norm.

Fiona jolted at the way he answered the phone.

"We can talk about that later. I told you I'm on my anniversary trip." A couple seconds of silence. "Yep. See you Tuesday."

Tyler ended the call.

"Tuesday?" She raised a brow.

"I'm taking Monday off too. We'll take the boys to the zoo when we get home." He swiped at the phone another time or two. "Airplane mode." He tossed it onto the nightstand.

As she grinned, he bowed at the waist, looking as dashing in faded pajama pants and a black T-shirt as he had in his pirate gear. "Now, my lady, where were we?"

"I believe, dear sir"—she dipped into a curtsy—"you were about to sweep me off my feet."

He scooped her into his arms, and they let the rest of the world drift away.

Epilogue

$\mathcal{M}$rs. Easley closed the door behind another happy couple and sent up a prayer of thanks for the job that had been her joy to perform these past decades. She doubted many others were blessed with the type of work she enjoyed, but who was she to say?

The Lord worked in his own ways.

Humming a tune from many years ago, she bustled down the hall and into the sunlit kitchen. In all her years at The Depot, this would be a first. She'd had guests in every room, and even a few who had gone to the tower room over the years. Once, a girl started her journey from the library. But never had anyone made use of the kitchen.

Special, indeed.

She checked the cabinets for all of the necessary ingredients and unearthed baking utensils from the drawers.

"Let's see…. That should be everything, I think." She chose a sunny-yellow apron and laid it on the counter next to the open book.

She flipped pages to the right spot.

"Ah. Here we are. Flour, sugar, eggs. Yes, I have those. An apron, yes." She snapped her fingers. "Right. The key ingredient for this concoction. It must be the right one."

She rummaged in a back drawer for what she needed. An antique hand mixer. She twisted the handle, and the gear turned smoothly, spinning the two whisks at the end.

"Perfect." She set the tool on the counter with the other items. "Now where did I put that old flapper dress?"

She'd better hurry. This one would arrive early.

The doorbell rang.

"Coming!" She bustled toward the door. No time to change. Oh well. She supposed she didn't need to.

The thought dissipated as a headband settled around her temples.

"Thank you, Father." She patted the glittering fringe on her dress. "You never cease to amaze, even after all this time."

Still humming the jaunty tune, she hurried to open the door to another adventure.

Dear reader,

I hope you enjoyed your trip to the Vanderbilt Ball with Tyler and Fiona. If you would take a few moments to leave a sentence or two about what you enjoyed online, I would greatly appreciate it.

Check out the series page for more Back Inn Time books. Coming soon!

Books by Stephenia H. McGee

Ironwood Family Saga
The Whistle Walk
Heir of Hope
Missing Mercy
*Ironwood Series Set
*Get the entire series at a discounted price

The Accidental Spy Series
*Previously published as The Liberator Series
An Accidental Spy
A Dangerous Performance
A Daring Pursuit
*Accidental Spy Series Set
*Get the entire series at a discounted price

Stand Alone Titles
In His Eyes
Eternity Between Us
The Cedar Key
The Secrets of Emberwild
The Swindler's Daughter

Time Travel

Her Place in Time
(Stand alone, but ties to Rosswood from
The Accidental Spy Series)

The Hope of Christmas Past
(Stand alone, but ties to Belmont from *In His Eyes*)

The Back Inn Time Series
Stand alone books that can be read in any order

Novellas

The Heart of Home

The Hope of Christmas Past

Buy direct from the author's online bookshop and
SAVE over every other retailer.
https://shop.stepheniamcgee.com
https://www.stepheniamcgee.com

About the Author

Stephenia H. McGee is a multi-published author of stories of faith, hope, and healing set in the Deep South. She lives in Mississippi, where she is a mom of two rambunctious boys, writer, dreamer, and husband spoiler. Her novel *The Cedar Key* was a 2021 Faith, Hope, and Love Readers' Choice award winner. A member of the ACFW (American Christian Fiction Writers) and the DAR (Daughters of the American Revolution), she loves all things books and history. Stephenia also loves connecting with readers and can often be found having fun with her Faithful Readers Team on Facebook. For more on books and upcoming events and to connect with Stephenia, visit her at www.StepheniaMcGee.com.

Visit her website at www.StepheniaMcGee.com and be sure to sign up for the newsletter to get sneak peeks, behind the scenes fun, the occasional recipe, and special giveaways.
Facebook: Stephenia H. McGee, Christian Fiction Author
Twitter: @StepheniaHMcGee
Instagram: stepheniahmcgee
Pinterest: Stephenia H. McGee

Buy direct from the author's online bookshop and SAVE over every other retailer.
https://shop.stepheniamcgee.com

Made in the USA
Columbia, SC
12 February 2025